Learning Resources Center
University of Wyoming Libraries

THE DOMINICAN AMERICANS

Senior Consulting Editor

Senator Daniel Patrick Moynihan

Consulting Editors

Ann Orlov
Managing Editor, Harvard Encyclopedia of American Ethnic Groups

M. Mark Stolarik
President, The Balch Institute for Ethnic Studies, Philadelphia

James F. Watts
Chairman, History Department, City College of New York

The Peoples of North America

THE DOMINICAN AMERICANS

Christopher Dwyer

CHELSEA HOUSE PUBLISHERS
New York Philadelphia

On the cover: Dominican-American students at Brandeis High School in New York City relax together at the end of the school day.

CHELSEA HOUSE PUBLISHERS
Editor-in-Chief: Remmel Nunn
Managing Editor: Karyn Gullen Browne
Copy Chief: Juliann Barbato
Picture Editor: Adrian G. Allen
Art Director: Maria Epes
Deputy Copy Chief: Mark Rifkin
Assistant Art Director: Loraine Machlin
Manufacturing Manager: Gerald Levine
Systems Manager: Rachel Vigier
Production Manager: Joseph Romano
Production Coordinator: Marie Claire Cebrián

The Peoples of North America
Senior Editor: Sean Dolan

Staff for THE DOMINICAN AMERICANS
Assistant Editor: Elise Donner
Copy Editor: Brian Sookram
Picture Research: PAR/NYC
Senior Designer: Noreen Romano
Cover Illustration: Paul Biniasz
Banner Design: Hrana Janto

Copyright © 1991 by Chelsea House Publishers, a division of Main Line Book Co. All rights reserved. Printed and bound in the United States of America.

3 5 7 9 8 6 4 2

Library of Congress Cataloging-in-Publication Data
Dwyer, Christopher.
 The Dominican Americans/Christopher Dwyer.
  p. cm.—(The Peoples of North America)
 Includes bibliographical references.
 Summary: Discusses the history, culture, and religion of the Dominican Americans, their place in American society, and the problems they face as an ethnic group in North America.
 ISBN 0-87754-872-2
    0-7910-0287-8 (pbk.)
 1. Dominican Americans—Juvenile literature. [1. Dominican Americans.] I. Title. II. Series.
E184.D6D89 1990 89-77421   CIP 973'.04687293—dc20
AC

CONTENTS

Introduction: A Nation of Nations	7
An Unseen Giant	13
The Land Columbus Loved	21
"No One Left to Close It"	37
Picture Essay: Chasing the Dream	49
En Nueva York	61
A World Apart	71
Baseball—Chasing the Dream	85
On to the Second Generation	105
Futher Reading	108
Index	109

THE PEOPLES OF NORTH AMERICA

THE IMMIGRANT EXPERIENCE	THE IBERIAN AMERICANS
ILLEGAL ALIENS	THE INDO-AMERICANS
IMMIGRANTS WHO RETURNED HOME	THE INDO-CHINESE AMERICANS
THE AFRO-AMERICANS	THE IRANIAN AMERICANS
THE AMERICAN INDIANS	THE IRISH AMERICANS
THE AMISH	THE ITALIAN AMERICANS
THE ARAB AMERICANS	THE JAPANESE AMERICANS
THE ARMENIAN AMERICANS	THE JEWISH AMERICANS
THE BALTIC AMERICANS	THE KOREAN AMERICANS
THE BULGARIAN AMERICANS	THE MEXICAN AMERICANS
THE CARPATHO-RUSYN AMERICANS	THE NORWEGIAN AMERICANS
THE CENTRAL AMERICANS	THE PACIFIC ISLANDERS
THE CHINESE AMERICANS	THE PEOPLES OF THE ARCTIC
THE CROATIAN AMERICANS	THE POLISH AMERICANS
THE CUBAN AMERICANS	THE PUERTO RICANS
THE CZECH AMERICANS	THE ROMANIAN AMERICANS
THE DANISH AMERICANS	THE RUSSIAN AMERICANS
THE DOMINICAN AMERICANS	THE SCOTCH-IRISH AMERICANS
THE DUTCH AMERICANS	THE SCOTTISH AMERICANS
THE ENGLISH AMERICANS	THE SERBIAN AMERICANS
THE FILIPINO AMERICANS	THE SLOVAK AMERICANS
THE FRENCH AMERICANS	THE SOUTH AMERICANS
THE FRENCH CANADIANS	THE SWEDISH AMERICANS
THE GERMAN AMERICANS	THE TURKISH AMERICANS
THE GREEK AMERICANS	THE UKRAINIAN AMERICANS
THE HAITIAN AMERICANS	THE WEST INDIAN AMERICANS
THE HUNGARIAN AMERICANS	

CHELSEA HOUSE PUBLISHERS

A NATION OF NATIONS

Daniel Patrick Moynihan

The Constitution of the United States begins: "We the People of the United States..." Yet, as we know, the United States is not made up of a single group of people. It is made up of many peoples. Immigrants from Europe, Asia, Africa, and Central and South America settled in North America seeking a new life filled with opportunities unavailable in their homeland. Coming from many nations, they forged one nation and made it their own. More than 100 years ago, Walt Whitman expressed this perception of America as a melting pot: "Here is not merely a nation, but a teeming Nation of nations."

Although the ingenuity and acts of courage of these immigrants, our ancestors, shaped the North American way of life, we sometimes take their contributions for granted. This fine series, *The Peoples of North America*, examines the experiences and contributions of the immigrants and how these contributions determined the future of the United States and Canada.

Immigrants did not abandon their ethnic traditions when they reached the shores of North America. Each ethnic group had its own customs and traditions, and each brought different experiences, accomplishments, skills, values, styles of dress, and tastes in food that lingered long after its arrival. Yet this profusion of differences created a singularity, or bond, among the immigrants.

The United States and Canada are unusual in this respect. Whereas religious and ethnic differences have sparked intolerance throughout the rest of the world—from the 17th-century religious wars to the 19th-century nationalist movements in Europe to the near extermination of the Jewish people under Nazi Germany—North Americans have struggled to learn how to respect each other's differences and live in harmony.

Millions of immigrants from scores of homelands brought diversity to our continent. In a mass migration, some 12 million immigrants passed through the waiting rooms of New York's Ellis Island; thousands more came to the West Coast. At first, these immigrants were welcomed because labor was needed to meet the demands of the Industrial Age. Soon, however, the new immigrants faced the prejudice of earlier immigrants who saw them as a burden on the economy. Legislation was passed to limit immigration. The Chinese Exclusion Act of 1882 was among the first laws closing the doors to the promise of America. The Japanese were also effectively excluded by this law. In 1924, Congress set immigration quotas on a country-by-country basis.

Such prejudices might have triggered war, as they did in Europe, but North Americans chose negotiation and compromise instead. This determination to resolve differences peacefully has been the hallmark of the peoples of North America.

The remarkable ability of Americans to live together as one people was seriously threatened by the issue of slavery. It was a symptom of growing intolerance in the world. Thousands of settlers from the British Isles had arrived in the colonies as indentured servants, agreeing to work for a specified number of years on farms or as apprentices in return for passage to America and room and board. When the first Africans arrived in the then-British colonies during the 17th century, some colonists thought that they too should be treated as indentured servants. Eventually, the question of whether the Africans should be viewed as indentured, like the English, or as slaves who could be owned for life, was considered in a Maryland court. The court's calamitous decree held that blacks were slaves bound to lifelong servitude, and so were their children. America went through a time of moral examination and civil war before it finally freed African slaves and their descendants. The principle that all people are created equal had faced its greatest challenge and survived.

Yet the court ruling that set blacks apart from other races fanned flames of discrimination that burned long after slavery was abolished—and that still flicker today. The concept of racism had existed for centuries in countries throughout the world. For instance, when the Manchus conquered China in the 13th century, they decreed that Chinese and Manchus could not intermarry. To impress their superiority on the conquered Chinese, the Manchus ordered all Chinese men to wear their hair in a long braid called a queue.

By the 19th century, some intellectuals took up the banner of racism, citing Charles Darwin. Darwin's scientific studies hypothesized that highly evolved animals were dominant over other animals. Some advocates of this theory applied it to humans, asserting that certain races were more highly evolved than others and thus were superior.

This philosophy served as the basis for a new form of discrimination, not only against nonwhite people but also against various ethnic groups. Asians faced harsh discrimination and were depicted by popular 19th-century newspaper cartoonists as depraved, degenerate, and deficient in intelligence. When the Irish flooded American cities to escape the famine in Ireland, the cartoonists caricatured the typical "Paddy" (a common term for Irish immigrants) as an apelike creature with jutting jaw and sloping forehead.

By the 20th century, racism and ethnic prejudice had given rise to virulent theories of a Northern European master race. When Adolf Hitler came to power in Germany in 1933, he popularized the notion of Aryan supremacy. *Aryan*, a term referring to the Indo-European races, was applied to so-called superior physical characteristics such as blond hair, blue eyes, and delicate facial features. Anyone with darker and heavier features was considered inferior.

Buttressed by these theories, the German Nazi state from 1933 to 1945 set out to destroy European Jews, along with Poles, Russians, and other groups considered inferior. It nearly succeeded. Millions of these people were exterminated.

The tragedies brought on by ethnic and racial intolerance throughout the world demonstrate the importance of North America's efforts to create a society free of prejudice and inequality.

A relatively recent example of the New World's desire to resolve ethnic friction nonviolently is the solution the Canadians found to a conflict between two ethnic groups. A long-standing dispute as to whether Canadian culture was properly English or French resurfaced in the mid-1960s, dividing the peoples of the French-speaking Quebec Province from those of the English-speaking provinces. Relations grew tense, then bitter, then violent. The Royal Commission on Bilingualism and Biculturalism was established to study the growing crisis and to propose measures to ease the tensions. As a result of the commission's recommendations, all official documents and statements from the national government's capital at Ottawa are now issued in both French and English, and bilingual education is encouraged.

The year 1980 marked a coming of age for the United States's ethnic heritage. For the first time, the U.S. Census asked people about their ethnic background. Americans chose from more than 100 groups, including French Basque, Spanish Basque, French Canadian, Afro-American, Peruvian, Armenian, Chinese, and Japanese. The ethnic group with the largest response was English (49.6 million). More than 100 million Americans claimed ancestors from the British Isles, which includes England, Ireland, Wales, and Scotland. There were almost as many Germans (49.2 million) as English. The Irish-American population (40.2 million) was third, but the next largest ethnic group, the Afro-Americans, was a distant fourth (21 million). There was a sizable group of French ancestry (13 million), as well as of Italian (12 million). Poles, Dutch, Swedes, Norwegians, and Russians followed. These groups, and other smaller ones, represent the wondrous profusion of ethnic influences in North America.

Canada, too, has learned more about the diversity of its population. Studies conducted during the French/English conflict showed that Canadians were descended from Ukrainians, Germans, Italians, Chinese, Japanese, native Indians, and Eskimos, among others. Canada found it had no ethnic majority, although nearly half of its immigrant population had come from the British Isles. Canada, like the United States, is a land of immigrants for whom mutual tolerance is a matter of reason as well as principle.

The people of North America are the descendants of one of the greatest migrations in history. And that migration is not over. Koreans, Vietnamese, Nicaraguans, Cubans, and many others are heading for the shores of North America in large numbers. This mix of cultures shapes every aspect of our lives. To understand ourselves, we must know something about our diverse ethnic ancestry. Nothing so defines the North American nations as the motto on the Great Seal of the United States: *E Pluribus Unum*—Out of Many, One.

Approximately 53 percent of the Dominican population lives in rural areas, yet only a small percentage of land is available to be worked. Parents of children such as this one from the central town of La Vega often have no choice but to emigrate in order to feed their family.

AN UNSEEN GIANT

On May 30, 1961, a light blue Chevrolet Bel Air sedan hurtled along a desolate stretch of coastal highway running west out of Ciudad Trujillo, capital of the Dominican Republic. Behind the wheel was a dark, powerful-looking chauffeur. Also in the car were 2 carbines, a revolver, a briefcase holding U.S. $110,000 and Dominican pesos, and the pale, freckled Jefe (chief) himself—Generalissimo Rafael Leónidas Trujillo Molina, who for 30 years had run the Dominican Republic as though it were his private estate. Indeed, by 1961 he owned, directly or indirectly, 60 percent of the nation's land.

The capital of the Dominican Republic had been called Santo Domingo for more than 400 years before it was renamed early in Trujillo's reign. And the capital city was not all that bore the generalissimo's name. Streets, parks, license plates, statues, bronze plaques, and even the country's highest mountain, Pico Trujillo, paid tribute to this man. Perhaps most dramatically, scores of blinking neon lights on the streets of the capital proclaimed "God and Trujillo."

Trujillo's ego and bloodlust were so great that even unsavory Latin American dictators such as Nicaragua's

Anastasio "Tacho" Somoza and Paraguay's Alfredo Stroessner kept their distance from this lavishly uniformed, heavyset, shrill-voiced tyrant. Known for his prodigious appetite for women, liquor, and power, Trujillo was on his way to visit a mistress this very night. But an organized group of his own government's officials, supported by the president of the United States and carrying untraceable weapons supplied by the U.S. Central Intelligence Agency (CIA), were determined that Trujillo would not reach his destination.

As the blue car whisked by the grounds of the Fair of Peace and Fraternity of the Free World, which Trujillo had built in 1954 at the cost of one-third of the country's annual budget, another Chevrolet pulled onto the highway and fell into the lane behind the dictator's car. Only the sound of the cars' engines and the far-off splashing of waves against the shore could be heard in the humid and still Caribbean night.

Suddenly, an explosion broke the stillness and the rear window of Trujillo's car was gone, shattered by gunfire. The driver slammed on the brakes and a stocky, gray-haired man in a green military uniform, brandishing a revolver, staggered from the rear of the blue Chevy. The assassins poured out of the black car now stopped behind Trujillo's. One of them pointed his gun directly at El Jefe and fired. Trujillo took several steps in one direction, turned, fell to his knees, and collapsed face forward. Rafael Trujillo, the self-proclaimed Benefactor of the Fatherland and Father of the New Fatherland, was dead, his body pierced by five bullets. The era of Trujillo had ended.

Trujillo's demise in 1961 marked the beginning of three decades of Dominican immigration to the United States. During the 31 years of his reign (1930–61), Trujillo tightly restricted movement out of the country; his death, along with political and economic troubles that have continued to the present day, initiated a flood of emigration. According to the Immigration and Naturalization Service (INS), whose figures do not

Newsmen examine the car in which Trujillo took his last ride. On May 30, 1961, Trujillo was assassinated on an isolated road near the capital city of Santo Domingo, which had been renamed Ciudad Trujillo by the dictator. His death unleashed further political and economic turmoil as well as a wave of immigration to Puerto Rico and the mainland United States.

include the many Dominicans who have entered the United States illegally, Dominican immigration rose from 756 people in 1960, Trujillo's last full year in power, to anywhere from 3,000 to nearly 20,000 in each of the years from 1961 through 1980. From 1969 on, more than 100,000 Dominicans entered the United States each year with a visitor's visa; it is impossible to say how many may have overstayed these visas and obtained jobs illegally. Even more difficult to estimate is the total number of Dominicans who have sneaked or been smuggled into the United States.

Although the Dominican Americans' story is still being written, a generation has passed since it began, a span of time in which the Dominican presence in the United States has grown from an insignificant one to that of an "unseen giant." In New York City, the Dominican population of 700,000 rivals the Puerto Rican and Cuban populations, traditionally the city's largest Latino groups in a total Latino population of 2 million.

The Dominican Republic is a Caribbean nation that occupies the eastern two-thirds of Hispaniola, the island just east of Cuba; the western third comprises the country of Haiti. Its 1989 population was estimated at about 7.3 million. Another 1 million Dominicans live in

In 1960, Dominican exiles in New York staged protests against the dictator Rafael Trujillo and his most recent attempt at eliminating political opposition. Although Trujillo forbade emigration, many Dominicans managed to escape his repressive rule.

the continental United States, predominantly in New York City, or in Puerto Rico, 75 miles to the east of Hispaniola.

The immigrant community of 700,000 in New York forms the largest Dominican population outside of Santo Domingo. Yet many New Yorkers are probably not even aware of this vast community and might be surprised to learn that in every year of the 1980s, the Dominican Republic supplied the city's largest group of immigrants. Americans' limited awareness of the Dominicans in their midst may be attributed to two causes. First, Americans often mistake Dominicans for Puerto Ricans; second, most of New York's Dominicans live in Manhattan's Washington Heights or in the Corona section of Queens, neighborhoods the average New Yorker rarely has occasion to visit.

Over the years, Dominican immigrants to the United States have proven to be an important source of income for the Dominican Republic itself. In 1987, the Dominican consulate reported that Dominican immigrants annually send $800 million home to their families. By contrast, U.S. foreign aid to the Dominican Republic in 1987 totaled a mere $62 million. It is clear that the Dominican Republic's most basic resource—its people—has proven more profitable and supportive than either economic development or foreign assistance.

For the Dominicans, immigration to the United States is more difficult than it is for the Puerto Ricans or the Cubans. They do not have the automatic U.S. citizenship that is conferred on Puerto Ricans at birth, nor do they enjoy the special status of Cubans, who may immigrate to the United States with a minimum of trouble if they claim to be "political refugees" from Fidel Castro's Communist regime. As a result, perhaps as many as half of New York's Dominicans are undocumented workers or illegal aliens, people without the documents that allow them to live permanently and work legally in the United States. The Dominican consulate estimates that only Mexico has more illegal aliens living in the United States.

U.S. immigration policy works to control legal immigration. The Immigration and Nationality Act of 1952 retained the exclusionary principle created by earlier legislation of considering national origins in fixing immigration quotas, a principle that favored people from northern and western European countries. However, the 1952 act did succeed in retaining and enlarging the nonquota class of immigrants, which includes the immediate relatives of U.S. citizens and of permanent residents and members of special categories, such as those with extraordinary educational or technical training. In 1965, at the start of the great wave of Dominican immigration, the United States passed the Hart-Celler Act, which abolished the unpopular national origins quota system and retained the nonquota admissions categories but fixed limits on the number of immigrants from Eastern and Western Hemisphere countries that would be welcome, favoring those from the Eastern Hemisphere. In 1976, the Western Hemisphere Act

Almost 30 years after Trujillo's death, thousands of Dominicans are analfabetos *(illiterates) and poor* campesinos *(countryfolk); thousands endure primitive living conditions, as does this La Vega resident, seen in 1985 bathing in a stream. Thousands emigrate each year in search of a better life.*

equalized this number and limited to 20,000 the number of visas granted to each country in each hemisphere. In places such as Mexico, the Dominican Republic, and Haiti—countries that border or are located extremely close to the United States and are home to many more people wanting to immigrate than the law now allows—people routinely devise stratagems for entering the United States outside of the legal channels.

The undocumented status of many Dominicans in the United States denies them most political and economic power. When an illegal Dominican immigrant asks for official help regarding housing, health care, education, or employment, he or she runs the risk of deportation. And the 1986 Immigration Reform and Control Act created for the first time a sharp delineation between illegal and legal employees in the workplace. Under the new law, employers are required to act as enforcers by examining and verifying citizenship documents when hiring an employee. Even if an employer takes the risk of employing an illegal Dominican, the worker pays a price. While Puerto Rican workers, as citizens, can insist on fair treatment, illegal Dominicans do not dare. Herman Badillo, a Puerto Rican and a former U.S. representative from New York City who worked on immigration issues while in Congress, remembers Dominican sweatshop workers telling him that they would like to vote in favor of a labor union, but that their bosses threatened to call in the INS, the federal agency responsible for regulating immigration, if they did.

Still, Dominicans from all educational and economic levels continue to come, legally or not. They seek refuge from an economic nightmare—60 percent average annual inflation rate, 25 percent unemployment, a $4 billion foreign debt—from which it seems their country cannot be roused. With good reason, the Dominican people associate elections and other political events with great uncertainty about their country's political and economic future. It seems that no matter who is in power, the problems remain. The election and rapid ouster of the Dominican Revolutionary party (PDR) candidate Juan Bosch in 1963, the first elections following the revolution of 1965, the election of Joaquín Balaguer and the Reformist party in 1974, and the election of the PDR's candidate in 1978 have all been followed by spurts in emigration. From the late 1960s through the late 1970s, even though the political situation was relatively stable and the economy on a rare upswing, thousands emigrated every year. As the words of "A Cibaoen in New York," a once-popular merengue (a type of Dominican folk ballad and dance form), attest, the grandiose claims of returning immigrants never fail to depict immigration as an irresistible prospect, even though the reality is often less appealing than the image:

They say Americans never speak of anything less than millions
And I said I would go and gather up the leftovers.
When I arrived there at dawn
I said, "This is a beautiful thing. I will become a Yankee!"
My family believes I am playing around and I was taken by the devil in New York.
My cousin Juan Maria met me at the airport.
Instead of inviting me for a drink he took me to a factory.
The little that I earn I send to my wife.
I earn 48 and send them 26.
My family believes I am playing around and I was taken by the devil in New York.
She wrote me right away that I had already begun to drink.
Of the bundle that I earn I send 26.
Everyone who comes from there, this is what they believe.
They think that dollar bills are to be gathered up on Broadway.

A late-15th-century woodcut from Giuliano Dati's La Lettera Dellisole, *from 1493, shows King Ferdinand of Spain pointing across the Atlantic Ocean to Christopher Columbus's landing on the island of Hispaniola in 1492. Four years later, Columbus's brother Bartholomeo, under the explorer's orders, founded the city of Santo Domingo.*

THE LAND COLUMBUS LOVED

Hispaniola, a 30,000-square-mile Caribbean island located about 575 miles southeast of Florida and today divided between the countries of Haiti and the Dominican Republic, was the locus of European colonists' grandest hopes and bitterest disappointments. The Dominican Republic's history is one of political chaos and economic misery. Its social system is in some ways still more suited to the Middle Ages than to the modern world, and the government's despoiling of the country's natural resources demonstrates little concern for the future. In the past three decades, the Dominican Republic's political instability and volatile economy have driven thousands of its citizens to the United States.

Colonial Masters

Hispaniola was discovered in 1492 by Christopher Columbus, an Italian mariner sponsored by the Spanish monarchs Ferdinand and Isabella. Columbus described it to his patrons as a kind of paradise—"[Hispaniola] is marvelous, the sierras and the mountains and the plains and the champaigns and the lands are so beautiful and fat for planting and sowing, and for livestock of every sort, and for building towns and cities"—and it became the site of the first Spanish colony in the Americas. In 1496, Columbus's brother Bartholomeo founded the first permanent city in the New World, Santo Domingo de Guzmán, on the island's southern coast; it was there that Spanish officials first put into place the institutions of government that Spain would use to control virtually an entire hemisphere. There, too, the conquistadores (conquerors) established the New World's first cathedral, hospital, and university, the University of Santo Domingo, authorized by King Philip II of Spain in 1558.

In 1558, King Philip II of Spain, shown here in a portrait by the Italian painter Titian, authorized the granting of degrees and the establishment of four faculties—philosophy, medicine, theology, and jurisprudence—at the University of Santo Domingo. The imposition of Spanish culture in the New World included the often forcible inculcation of Catholicism.

Spanish mistreatment of the native peoples of the Americas was notorious, as illustrated in this 16th-century print. Within 30 years of Spanish occupation, the native Indian population of Hispaniola was virtually wiped out.

And it was in Hispaniola that the Spanish carried out their first, deadly rout of the native peoples of the Americas. Between 200,000 and 600,000 Taino Indians had occupied Hispaniola before Columbus's arrival. Fewer than 30 years later, essentially none remained. Deliberate massacres, starvation, epidemics, overwork, and the demoralized Indians' reluctance to bring children into a life of Spanish-imposed slavery all contributed to this devastation.

For a time, Santo Domingo flourished as an administrative center and a jumping-off point for further Spanish exploration, but its importance diminished once the conquistadores discovered the fabulous wealth of Mexico and Peru. In 1603, the Spanish monarch Philip III, determined to retain total control over his empire's trade, became furious at the colonists' export of cowhides—Santo Domingo's major agricultural product—to other nations. (Santo Domingo was the name of the Spanish colony on Hispaniola as well as the name of its capital city.) Philip ordered that Hispaniola's inhabitants be removed to the island's much less fertile southeastern section. In doing so,

Spain quashed Hispaniola's modest economic growth and left it vulnerable to invasion. Reachable only over rough seas and with nothing to offer traders, Santo Domingo's most frequent visitors were notorious Caribbean pirates and French invaders seeking to expand the French colony of Saint-Domingue on Hispaniola's western shore.

The colony's social structure was made up of a handful of nobles at the top, a small middle class of artisans and craftspeople, and a vast population of desperately poor peasants. Because Spain's primary concern was siphoning off the island's natural wealth, over time it showed little interest in introducing social and economic reforms. As a result, the majority of colonists could hope for no improvement in either their economic status (in the form of gaining their own land) or their political fortunes (in the form of self-government or democracy). Even today, the Dominican economy is more oriented toward producing exports for the world market than toward feeding the Dominican people, and the class structure is similar in its rigidity to that of centuries past.

Waning Power

As the Spanish Empire weakened throughout the 17th and 18th centuries, so did Spanish control of the Caribbean. France gradually claimed an ever-greater portion of Hispaniola, which it called Saint-Domingue. While Spanish settlers scraped out a meager living in the east, with the help of a relatively small African slave population, Saint-Domingue became the world's richest colony, its economy driven by huge infusions of French government money and the labor of some 500,000 slaves. (The free white population was only 70,000.) To some extent, Saint-Domingue's thriving economy helped support Santo Domingo. The French possession supplied the world market with sugar, coffee, cotton, and indigo; Santo Domingo sold cattle, horses, tobacco, and wood to its prosperous neighbor.

In this 18th-century print, a flamboyantly attired Spanish soldier of fortune, or hidalgo, *is attended by a black slave. Africans were brought to Santo Domingo in the 18th century to serve its population of Spanish adventurers. The Spanish colony, however, had far fewer African slaves than did its French neighbor, Saint-Domingue.*

By 1795, France's control of the island was so complete and its power in Europe so great in comparison with Spain's that the Spanish ceded it all of Hispaniola, but France would govern its new colony only briefly. Inspired by the ideals of the ongoing French Revolution—liberty, equality, fraternity—the mulattoes (people of mixed white and black ancestry) and slaves of Saint-Domingue rose in revolt. In the course of years of warfare, the former slaves defeated in succession their white colonial overlords and the French, Spanish, and British armies. The war ended in 1804 with the founding of Haiti, Latin America's first independent republic.

In the meantime, Santo Domingo continued to decline economically, and 40,000 white Spanish settlers left the island. By 1822, following a brief interlude of independence for Spanish Haiti, as Santo Domingo was then called, Haiti controlled the entire island of Hispaniola. The former Spanish colony was in ruins, its natural resources thoroughly plundered and half its people lost to emigration or death during the previous 30 years. The destruction of the Indian population had wiped out any native tradition, and Santo Domingo's isolation ensured that it was bypassed, as historian Howard J. Wiarda has written, "by all the great and far-reaching revolutions of the modern world.... [Santo Domingo's] intellectual, religious, economic, and political traditions and institutions remained rooted not in the modern but in the medieval era." Even in February 1844, when it became independent of Haiti, the new "Dominican Republic" was hardly unified. It remained a collection of squabbling military factions, its people passive as a result of eras of dictatorship, its corrupt leaders notoriously susceptible to foreign influence.

During the 22 years of Haitian rule, many whites continued to flee the Dominican Republic, while "freedmen," blacks and mulattoes who had bought their freedom, became the social equals of the Europeans who remained. This period of social transition was critical in the development of the Dominican people. After the declaration of Dominican independence on February 27, 1844, people of color and their descendants, not whites, largely controlled the fate of the former Spanish colony.

Independence and Oppression

From 1844 through 1916, a succession of dictators dominated the Dominican Republic, an ominous foreshadowing of the reign of Trujillo, whose absolute rule from 1930 to 1961 differed from that of his predecessors only in its thoroughness, rapaciousness, cleverness, and longevity. These dictators established the tradition of *personalismo*, in which political authority emanates from the charisma and heroism of a particular individual. This period also saw the entrenchment of the patterns of revolution, civil war, and the violent contention for political power that have since characterized Dominican politics.

For the first 30 years of the republic's life, General Pedro Santana, its first president, and Buenaventura Báez, devoted their successive turns in office to establishing the Dominican Republic as the protectorate of a major power such as the United States, France, or England, an arrangement that would fill both the Dominican treasury and their own pockets with quick profits. However, except for a brief interlude of Spanish control, their dream of a foreign-controlled Dominican Republic, in which they would serve as "administrators," never materialized.

The regimes of Ulises Heureaux and Ramon Cáceres, along with interludes of chaos that followed the assassinations of both of these leaders, brought the Dominican Republic up to 1916. Heureaux, like Báez and Santana before him, had borrowed large sums from the United States and various European countries. In 1904, the United States expressed its belief that it ought to be the sole agent involved in collecting the Dominican Republic's delinquent payments. In 1905, at the instigation of President Theodore Roosevelt, the United States and the Dominican Republic signed an agreement whereby the United States was to administer all finances and to collect all customs, setting aside a portion for repayment of foreign debts. In 1914, after the assassination of President Cáceres and the resignation of the succeeding president, Archbishop Adolfo A. Nouel, the United States announced its intention to restore peace and to establish a constitutional government in the Dominican Republic, even if it involved the use of American armed forces.

Two years later, the United States made good its threat and occupied the Dominican Republic. For the next eight years the U.S. Marines, under the command of Captain Harry S. Knapp, administered a military government. Knapp suspended the Dominican congress and, in the opinion of many, set himself up as a dictator. The marines restricted the Dominicans' freedoms while terrorizing them through a series of unprovoked atrocities.

The American military occupation had a decisive and long-lasting impact on the Dominican people. First, it planted in many people an intense distaste for the United States, which came to be seen as a colossus that under the guise of a concern for democracy had brought only insensitivity and repression to the country. This feeling of distrust has persisted and may partially explain why so many Dominican immigrants are determined to return to the Dominican Republic after making their fortunes in America.

Second, the occupation introduced an extensive American commercial presence to the Dominican Republic, the effects of which were as economically devastating as any scheme devised by Báez or Santana. American investment did provide the Dominicans with some jobs on construction and public-works projects to build roads, and the American presence was responsible for increased educational opportunities and the introduction of certain enjoyable American customs, such as baseball, into Dominican culture, but ultimately it was the Americans who benefited most from the occupation, not the Dominican people, in whose interests the invasion had been carried out. In 1924, the year that the U.S. occupation ended, Dominican companies owned only 9,568 acres of the land suitable for the cultivation of sugar, the island's most lucrative export. U.S. sugar companies owned 37 times as much, or 355,854 acres. This imbalance in the distribution of natural resources and wealth certainly played a major part in creating the

Trujillo as he appeared in 1939, on the eve of his first trip to the United States, during which he visited the World's Fair in New York. Alastair Reid, an American writer who lives in the Dominican Republic, says that "the dictator's shadow is still a deep and dense one" over the Dominican people.

economic malaise that continues to drive Dominicans to the United States.

Third, and perhaps most critical in the long run, the occupying marines, charged with reorganizing and professionalizing the armed forces, created a unified constabulary. This so-called National Army—never called into action except against its own people—played the crucial role in Rafael Trujillo's rise to the presidency in 1930 and in enabling him to maintain his iron grip on power for the next 30 years. Dominican nationalist Noel Henríquez has called Trujillo the "bastard son of the occupation forces."

Dominican immigration to North America is a relatively new phenomenon that began in large numbers only with Trujillo's death in 1961. The Trujillo era then—during which emigration was forbidden—and its aftermath are the periods of Dominican history most immediately relevant to those Dominicans in America today.

El Jefe

From 1930 to 1961, a people that had already seen its country wracked by economic troubles, internal political strife, and foreign occupation experienced the longest and most thorough dictatorship in its history. Trujillo wielded absolute power over virtually every aspect of Dominican society. He enjoyed total control over the armed forces and constantly shuffled military personnel from post to post so that no officer could build up a personal following loyal enough to overthrow him. El Jefe also established an extensive network of secret police that, by means of brainwashing, torture, and murder, silenced the voices of those opposed to his regime. Even Dominicans as far away as Puerto Rico, Havana, and New York were not beyond the reach of his henchmen.

Under Trujillo, freedoms guaranteed by the Dominican constitution did not exist in practice, and elections, though held regularly, were rigged to assure that El Jefe and his associates were victorious. He even amended the constitution to allow the president to succeed himself. The combination of state terror and wholesale prohibition of political participation effectively muzzled political activism throughout the 30 years of Trujillo's reign, turning an already docile population virtually apathetic. By 1961, many Dominicans with the means to do so had come to consider exile as the only escape from the ongoing oppression.

Trujillo considered himself the *patrón*, or father figure, of his country. True to the metaphor, he controlled the vast majority of the country's financial and material wealth, dispensing it a bit at a time for only those projects and causes that he considered worthwhile. For a while, the Dominican Republic profited from his paternalism. By 1941, Trujillo had succeeded in ending U.S. control in the Dominican Republic, and by 1947 he had completely repaid the nation's foreign debt; in fact, until the 1950s, the Dominican economy prospered. Trujillo used government money to finance the expansion of the military and to build extensive public works that improved communication and travel throughout the country. But by 1955, recession, unemployment, and huge government deficits, caused in part by Trujillo's

In December 1962, Juan Bosch and the Dominican Revolutionary party (PDR), a moderate left-of-center group, won the presidential election with the widespread support of campesinos and urban workers. The PDR's program emphasized economic development, social reform, and democratic freedom. Bosch (right) is seen here conferring with American newspaper columnist Drew Pearson.

U.S. military police search Dominicans at a crossing in Santo Domingo in 1965. When President Juan Bosch was forced to flee to Puerto Rico after a military coup, U.S. troops landed in the Dominican Republic, ostensibly to protect U.S. citizens. Continuing a long tradition of American involvement in Dominican affairs, the Central Intelligence Agency played an important role in the establishment of a coalition government to replace Bosch.

habit of siphoning off much of the government's money through various self-serving schemes, had brought misery to the majority of Dominicans. At the time of his death, the dictator's personal fortune was estimated at $800 million, while the income of the majority of Dominicans was negligible. Trujillo and his relatives owned 50 to 60 percent of the nation's arable land, and Trujillo-owned companies accounted for perhaps 80 percent of the volume of business in the capital. One historian wrote at the time that "it is impossible to eat, drink, smoke or dress without somehow benefiting *el benefactor* or his family. The Dominican pays him tribute from birth to death." With the outlook for freedom and economic independence so bleak, escape abroad seemed the only solution for many Dominicans of both the lower and the middle class.

Meet the New Boss

Although the Dominican people's initial reaction to Trujillo's death in 1961 was one of euphoria, years of political disorder, culminating in the crushing of the April 1965 revolution led by the Dominican Revolutionary party (PDR), most of the armed forces, and the people of Santo Domingo, demolished hopes for democracy or economic revival. (Again, the United States played a role. President Lyndon Johnson sent U.S. troops to the Dominican Republic to restore order, and the CIA played a large role in establishing an interim government there.) Frightened by the chaos and free of Trujillo's restrictions on emigration, middle-class Dominicans left the country in large numbers. Control of the government alternated among former Trujillo supporter Joaquín Balaguer, democrat Juan Bosch, and various groups of civilian and military leaders. In 1966, Balaguer defeated Bosch and the PDR and with the help of U.S. aid, high sugar prices, and new wealth from mineral resources, was able to stay in power until 1978. Balaguer's regime shared many traits with that of Trujillo, in particular, a hatred of communism and a reliance on the police and armed forces to crush domestic dissent. Lured by stories of easy wealth in the United States, people continued to emigrate, though most still intended to return to the Dominican Republic.

Emigration increased in the late 1970s and early 1980s as a result of a downturn in the Dominican

U.S. vice-president Hubert Humphrey (right) offers a toast to newly elected president Joaquín Balaguer, the Reformist party candidate, in July 1966.

economy brought about by a drop in the price of sugar and an increase in oil prices. Many of those who left the Dominican Republic at that time intended never to return; many others became temporary immigrants, spending part of each year working in the United States and returning home when they had saved some money. The economic slump coincided with the rise to power of the PDR, which held the presidency from 1978 to 1986. The PDR had long been respected for its commitment to democracy. Salvador Jorge Blanco, who served as president from 1982 to 1986, succeeded in eliminating much of the repression and corruption of the Trujillo and Balaguer years, but the attitude of many

In August 1982, outgoing president Jacobo Majluta Azar (left) was photographed with his successor, Jorge Blanco. Blanco's democratic government remained in power until 1986, during which time it corrected many of the wrongs perpetrated by both Trujillo and Balaguer; unfortunately, it was not successful in reviving the stagnant Dominican economy.

In May 1986, election workers update statistics for a television broadcast of balloting results. The election brought the return of Balaguer to the office of the presidency, but emigration did not diminish during his term.

Dominicans was summed up in the words of Reyna Reyes, a recent immigrant: "You can't eat democracy." By 1986, Balaguer was back in power, but the burdens of foreign debt, austerity measures imposed by the International Monetary Fund in its provision of aid, and a lack of jobs for the country's workers have continued to be serious problems, and the promise of wealth for those who can reach America has continued to lure the nation's people away.

In September 1986, the U.S. Coast Guard picked up 37 Dominican refugees from a 30-foot boat near Longboat Key, Florida. In spite of sophisticated technology and increased patrols, the Immigration and Naturalization Service (INS) has not been able to significantly affect the flow of illegal Dominican immigration to America.

"NO ONE LEFT TO CLOSE IT"

As night fell on September 4, 1980, the *Regina Express*, a Panamanian freighter commanded by an American captain and manned by a Dominican crew, was moored at a dock in Santo Domingo. It was scheduled to sail for Miami, Florida, the next day. As dockworkers headed home at the end of a full day's work in Santo Domingo's busy and historic port, the piers grew quiet.

Several hours passed. A warm Caribbean breeze, tinged just slightly with the odor of the city's polluted harbor, floated gently over Santo Domingo as people retired to their beds for the night. In the darkness, only a careful observer could have seen the men, 34 in all, who hastily began boarding the *Regina Express*. They moved as quietly as they could, but for these hardworking peasants with little experience as lawbreakers, sneaking on board a 1,500-ton freighter as stowaways in the middle of the night was an unfamiliar and disconcerting experience. Nevertheless, having invested their life savings and more in this journey, they hurried onto the vessel that would carry them to a better life several hundred miles across the Caribbean Sea.

It was not detection by the ship's crew that the men were trying to avoid. No, word had gotten out in Santo Domingo that for between $1,500 and $3,000, anyone wanting to escape the country could obtain illegal but secure passage to the United States mainland aboard the *Regina Express*. No need to brave, in an overloaded fishing trawler, the shark-filled waters of the stormy Mona Passage on a trip to Puerto Rico, from where one might or might not be able to obtain passage to New York. People said the *Regina Express* set a course straight for the promised land. And because the story had become more exaggerated each time it was told, men like Félix Tavarez, Rafael Flores, Augustin Genal Flores, and Alfredo Cáceres came to believe that everything from new clothes and taxi rides to documents and jobs would be waiting for them when they arrived in Miami.

When the group had boarded, a crew member instructed them to hide for just a few minutes in a ballast tank, an airtight container that serves to stabilize a ship by filling with seawater when the load is light and then by emptying when the load is heavy. Worried that the men might ignore his instructions to remain in the tank, the crew member locked it shut. But before long the tank began to fill with water, and the supply of air in the sealed compartment began to run short.

At the very moment the men were piling into the tank, Dominican navy officials, tipped off that illegal immigrants would be aboard the *Regina Express*, had begun a search of the upper decks of the ship. When the officials finally came to the ballast tank, they were startled to hear the panicked pounding and shouting of people trapped inside. The tank was drained and opened, but not before tragedy had struck. Of the 34 men who had boarded, only 12 were alive. Among the victims were Félix Tavarez, Rafael Flores, Augustin Genal Flores, and Alfredo Cáceres.

Félix Tavarez, a carpenter and home builder from Valverde, had been unable to find work for five years. He had hoped that in the United States he could earn enough money to send his youngest child to college. Tavarez had mortgaged the small house he had built to raise the $2,800 for the voyage.

Rafael Flores, a farmer also from Valverde, had sold his farm, his cows, and his house in order to collect enough money for the journey. His two young daughters, who stayed behind, were left with nothing. Flores's cousin, Augustin Genal Flores, had sold a bit of land and mortgaged his mother's home to pay for his chance to emigrate.

Alfredo Cáceres, who earned $20 a week selling lottery tickets, had first lost $1,800 in borrowed money to a man who falsely claimed he could provide passage to the United States. Cáceres then heard about the *Regina Express* and borrowed another $1,800 to finance the trip, even though his sister Veridiana had warned him against the trip, saying, "Brother, don't go, your children will be orphans."

Illegal Immigration

In 1980 alone, 60,000 Dominicans applied for some kind of visa to travel to the United States. Of these requests, approximately 40 percent—about 24,000 people—were rejected. As a result, a large number of Dominicans began to seek (and to find) ways to enter the United States illegally. It is in the context of this illegal immigration that the real drama of the Dominican Americans' story lies.

It is now 1986. An INS agent passing the time in a Santo Domingo bar encounters a husky Dominican who, with his cold eyes, trimmed goatee, and wispy hair piled back in a gentle widow's peak, looks more than a little satanic. The face is familiar; the agent has seen it before in photographs. It is Ramon Emilio Santana Camacho—known simply as Camacho—the 40-year-old head of an organization that between 1976 and 1987 smuggled 30,000 illegal immigrants into the United States. Camacho, not realizing that the man he is talking to is an INS agent, buys his new friend a drink and poses for a picture with him. Camacho remains at large.

In the past 50 years, the Dominican population has increased almost fivefold; fully 40 percent of the population is illiterate. Inadequate education and public health care, urban housing on the order of these shacks along Santo Domingo's Ozama River, and Hispaniola's relative proximity to the United States make emigration a likely choice for thousands of Dominicans each year.

In the years between the *Regina Express* tragedy and the INS agent's chance encounter with this trafficker in human lives, a succession of governments was unable to revive the Dominican Republic's sputtering economy. For Camacho and the other select few in his line of work, this did not mean unemployment, ruinous debt, and desperate measures, as it had for Félix Tavarez, Rafael Flores, Augustin Genal Flores, and Alfredo Cáceres. For those who made a dangerous and desperate living finding new ways of eluding the immigration authorities, the period was one of fabulous opportunity—a time of big risks but big payoffs. Over the last few decades, Dominicans have found several avenues through which to enter U.S. territory illegally. Some illegal immigrants, such as the men on the *Regina Express*, buy passage or sneak onto cargo ships sailing directly to the United States. As recently as September 1988, seven Dominican stowaways were discovered hiding on a ship that had just docked at a New Jersey port. Others manage to get only as far as Mexico by boat and then cross the border into Texas; from there, they are taken to New York. As with other schemes of illegal entry, this one is never guaranteed. In one notable 1981 case, the New York City police seized a filthy, garbage-filled tractor-trailer that had been used to bring illegal Dominicans from El Paso, Texas, to New York.

For the overwhelming majority of illegals, the path to the golden door leads across the Mona Passage to Puerto Rico, just 70 miles to the east of Hispaniola. In late 1986, the INS estimated that 1,000 Dominicans per month entered Puerto Rico this way, many braving the shark-filled passage in barely seaworthy smugglers' boats. Once in Puerto Rico, these illegal immigrants either continue on to the United States mainland, often by plane, or settle in the "Stop 15" area of Santurce, a dangerous and run-down section of San Juan, Puerto Rico's capital city. The men find work as mechanics or as construction laborers; women generally find jobs as housekeepers or cooks at food stands. For Dominicans, accustomed to making less than $1.00 an hour (on average, only about $85.00 per month), the U.S. minimum wage of $3.35 an hour seems princely by comparison. It is estimated that anywhere from 150,000 to 300,000 legal and illegal Dominicans are currently living in Puerto Rico.

For $500, a Dominican wanting only to reach Puerto Rico can simply be dropped off on the island's west coast. But if he is willing to spend more — perhaps as much as $5,000 — the traveler can expect transportation to San Juan, false documents, an airline ticket to New York, and an escort to guide him around immigration authorities at San Juan airport. Because Dominicans resemble Puerto Ricans, particularly in the eyes of

Since American businessmen erected sugar-processing mills in the Dominican Republic at the turn of the century, Dominicans have found backbreaking and low-paying employment in the sugarcane fields and factories. On the average, Dominican workers earn less than $1 an hour; Puerto Rico's minimum wage of $3.35 an hour and the promise of steady work are enticements few can ignore.

Dominican women inspect bananas in a processing plant. In spite of the land's natural bounty, poor agricultural methods and long-standing economic injustices make hunger an all-too-frequent part of Dominicans' lives. Myths of American prosperity are reinforced by the exaggerated success stories of relatives and friends who have emigrated.

Americans, it is often relatively easy for them to gain entry to the United States. (As U.S. citizens, Puerto Ricans do not require passports to enter the United States from their home island.)

Camacho's organization—run today by his lieutenants—provided emigrants with a 26-hour boat ride starting in tiny Agua Santa del Yuna, leading down a river to the sea, and finally across the treacherous Mona Passage to Puerto Rico. Camacho even offered his clients a guarantee of his services: If his passengers were caught and deported upon arrival in Puerto Rico, Camacho's men would take them across again at no charge.

In providing this guarantee, Camacho differed from just about every other smuggler offering a trip to U.S. territory. The Mona Passage has some of the roughest seas in the Caribbean. In stormy weather, many operators throw their passengers overboard or abandon them either on Mona Island or on one of the other uninhabitable, rocky islands between the Dominican Republic and Puerto Rico. Voyagers who are set down on Mona Island, where Puerto Rico's Department of Natural Resources maintains a station, can expect some food and water before being sent back to the Dominican

Republic. Passengers marooned on one of the other islands frequently die of starvation or dehydration while awaiting rescue. Some unscrupulous smugglers leave the Dominican Republic at night and drop off their boatload of passengers on another part of Hispaniola, only pretending to have made the crossing.

At least those who are duped in such a way live to try again. Hundreds of Dominicans have been killed in disasters like the one of December 1986, in which at least 16 Dominicans drowned after their boat capsized just a few hundred yards from the Puerto Rican seaside town of Rincón, an area known among surfers for its huge, powerful waves. The most notorious Mona Passage tragedy of recent years was the product of a tragic combination of mechanical failure and human indifference.

Around two o'clock in the morning on October 6, 1987, a 50-foot wooden fishing boat set out from Death's Head Beach in Nagua, a town along the eastern coast of the Dominican Republic about 110 miles north of Santo Domingo. Its passengers were 150 to 170 Dominicans, mostly women, each of whom had paid as much as $600 to sail across the Mona Passage to Puerto Rico. Surviving passengers later attested that the boat started taking on water as soon as it left Nagua. Three to four miles out, the boat's two outboard motors exploded. Many of the passengers could not swim and drowned immediately. But those who could swim, or who stayed afloat by hanging on to empty gasoline tanks and pieces of the boat, faced an even more gruesome fate.

About 30 members of this group somehow managed to fight their way back to land. Among these was a man named Rubio, who reached the shore at Nagua by morning and reported the disaster. But the other survivors were pulled by the powerful current as far out as 20 miles into shark-infested waters. The Dominican Republic civil defense director Eugenio Cabral's call for military rescue helicopters went unheeded for hours. Frustrated by the official indifference to the plight of these people, Cabral located a private plane and set out himself to pinpoint the survivors' location.

He came upon a grisly scene. Dozens of frantic swimmers were completely surrounded by more than 40 sharks, each weighing between 600 and 800 pounds. Eventually, military helicopters pulled about 32 people from the sea, but because Cabral's little plane could not put down on water, he was forced to watch helplessly as the swimmers were thrown into the air and then torn apart by the frenzied sharks. A companion, Puerto Rican civil defense director Luis Rolón Nevárez, described the scene: "There were several schools of about 15 sharks each, just attacking the refugees in the water. The sea was red around them. I've never seen anything more horrible." Cabral lamented, "It was just unbearable not being able to do anything for them."

Even though the tremendous Dominican influx into Puerto Rico had been apparent as early as 1980, during most of the decade the U.S. immigration authorities, preoccupied with Cuban and Haitian refugees headed for Florida, did not increase the resources available for halting illegal Dominican immigration. The INS's San Juan office was ill equipped to pick up and deport illegal Dominicans in Puerto Rico. The agency had no detention facility for captured illegals and no planes or boats for use in enforcing immigration law. In the mid-1980s, fewer than 15 percent of illegal Dominicans were being caught, and for a number of months during 1986,

Juan Mendez, a Dominican, leaves the INS office in Puerto Rico. Dominicans residing in Puerto Rico illegally have succeeded in receiving benefits from social programs; on an island where 60 percent of the population is eligible for food stamps, the illegal Dominican population has put a great strain on government services.

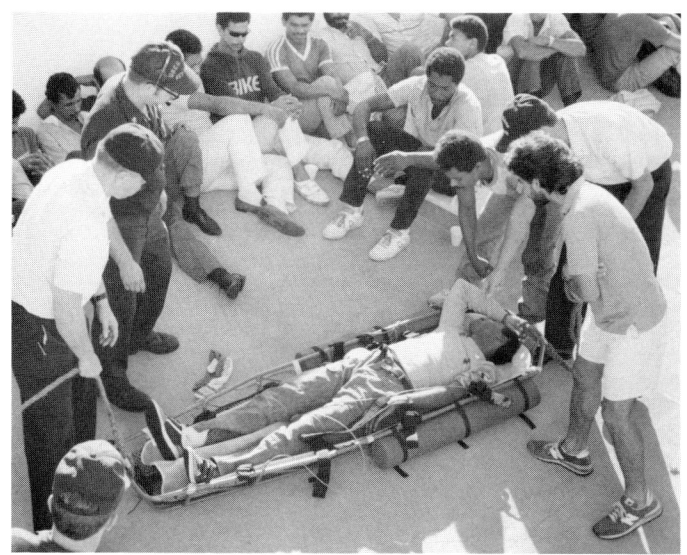

Members of the Coast Guard attend to a 26-year-old Dominican refugee, one of the 37 men picked up near Longboat Key, Florida, after he complained of severe stomach pains. The man was taken to a hospital, from which he later escaped. Apparently, his pains were merely a desperate, last-minute ploy to gain entry to the United States.

the INS did not even have enough money to feed the detainees, much less to send them back to the Dominican Republic. As a result, the hundreds of Dominicans who had been picked up were simply released and instructed to return to their country voluntarily within 30 days or else to appear for a deportation hearing. Not surprisingly, most Dominicans did neither.

The INS finally addressed the situation in October 1987, when it opened the first U.S. Border Patrol station outside the continental United States at the former Ramsey Air Force Base on the waters of the Mona Passage. Staffed by 15 officers and equipped with a plane and 2 boats, the post was the first of several planned for Puerto Rico's west coast. But at the same time, in response to the INS's action and to the Dominican navy's increased patrols of the Mona Passage, smugglers were developing a new route into Puerto Rico. The smugglers flew Dominicans and Haitians to the island of Saint Martin, which can be entered without a visa. Once there, immigrants boarded boats for a ride to a spot on Puerto Rico's less crowded and less frequently patrolled eastern coast.

Legal Immigration

Emigration from the Dominican Republic to the United States has always been fraught with risk. It is always expensive and, for those who attempt an illegal entry, often dangerous. Nevertheless, the Dominicans regard every new legal barrier to emigration as a new challenge to be overcome. Legal immigration to the United States has developed a folklore all its own.

Since the passing of the Immigration Act of 1924, the legislation that provided for a national origins system favoring northern and western Europeans, the United States has attempted to stem the flow of new immigrants across its borders. In the service of this goal, a complex set of laws, regulations, and administrative procedures have come to govern the immigration process. Currently, there are two types of visas available to foreign travelers to the United States: an immigrant and a nonimmigrant visa. With a nonimmigrant visa, easier to obtain, a potential foreign tourist or student receives permission to stay in the United States for a limited period of time.

An immigrant visa, on the other hand, confers "permanent resident" status on the holder. It has no time limit and entitles a foreigner to work for pay and to enjoy most of the rights of a U.S. citizen. With the passing of the Hart-Celler Act in 1965 (which went into effect in 1968), these visas became harder to obtain. The act stated that no more than 120,000 visas could be awarded anually to countries of the Western Hemisphere; in 1976, the Western Hemisphere Act established a limit of 20,000 visas per country. This unrealistic limitation has dramatically extended the period of time that even a qualified Dominican must wait for a visa. In general, immigrant visas are almost impossible to secure unless the applicant has a spouse, parent, or child who is already a permanent resident or citizen of the United States.

The complex process of applying for an immigrant visa has prompted Dominicans, often distrustful of government authorities, to develop an extensive, informal support system that provides such services as help with filling out forms, the carrying of messages and packages to relatives in the United States, and passage (legal or illegal) to Puerto Rico or New York.

One important link in this system is the visa broker. These brokers, who may also be travel agents or moneylenders, are part of an established tradition in the Dominican Republic, that of the *tributario* or *corredor*, an individual who helps Dominican citizens overcome the intricacies and sluggish pace at which government tends to work. An American citizen who had to obtain a national identity card, or *cédula*, because of a prolonged stay in the Dominican Republic, describes his experience with such a broker: "For a payment of 50 cents the tributario filled out the necessary form for me and then escorted me past waiting lines . . . into the inner office of the director where the application was handled expeditiously."

Dominican visa brokers are not only found in Santo Domingo. In New York City, the destination of most Dominican immigrants, visa brokers, who are often lawyers, provide help translating the English-language forms and guiding the immigrant through the U.S. government bureaucracy. New York is also home to many Dominican service agencies that provide transportation arrangements, referrals to visa brokers, and the cash to pay for these services. The relative ease with which family members may obtain visas under the current immigration law has led to a host of schemes—some illegal, others unethical—designed to meet the law's requirements. For example, a 23 year old's birth certificate might be altered so that the person can claim to be a "dependent," a status for which one must be under 19. In another instance, a potential immigrant may pay hundreds of dollars to be married to a

Dominican living legally in the United States so that he or she can gain legal entry into the country.

Another common method of entering the United States is through labor certification, a process in which immigrants may enter with the U.S. Department of Labor's certification that a certain type of worker is in short supply, either in the long term or temporarily. Employers in the United States may take the initiative by notifying the Department of Labor about a shortage of a particular type of worker and may request the labor of a group of aliens or even of a particular alien.

The possibility of being admitted into the United States through labor certification has spawned a host of arrangements for entry. Family members already in the United States often use brokers to find employers willing to sign statements certifying their need for a particular Dominican worker. A Dominican woman may come to the United States, work illegally for an employer for a period of time—as a live-in maid, for example—and then return to the Dominican Republic, where she will base her application for a residence visa on her employer's formal request for her return.

The *Typical* Dominican Immigrant

For years there has been some controversy over what constitutes the "typical" Dominican immigrant. Because the Dominican population in the United States has only recently become sizable, and because most Dominicans, especially illegal ones, tend not to participate in local politics, it is difficult to generalize about the background of Dominican immigrants in the United States.

There are, however, some truths about the Dominican people that may help Americans understand these relatively new immigrants. Dominicans in America may be surprised by a democratic society's reliance on drawing religious and racial lines to organize its people. While Dominicans have had to

(continued on page 57)

CHASING THE DREAM

The most visible success achieved by Dominicans in North America has been attained on the playing fields of the 26 American major league baseball teams. Slugger Pedro Guerrero (overleaf), a native of the baseball-mad Dominican city of San Pedro de Macorís, is one of the game's best clutch hitters, but Dominican ballplayers are best known for the grace and flair they exhibit at shortstop. Rafael Santana (right) and Julio Franco (above), both shortstops, are just 2 of the 26 Dominicans who held spots on major league rosters in the spring of 1990.

The vast majority of Dominican immigrants in the United States have settled in New York City, where they have transformed neighborhoods such as Washington Heights (upper left). At lower left, a Dominican softball player pauses for some nourishment during a picnic held in New York City's Central Park. As has been true for many immigrant groups before them, the success of Dominican Americans as a group in the United States will depend on how quickly they master English. Above, a group of Dominican students attend an English-as-a-second-language class at Lehman College in the Bronx.

Most Dominicans work at less glamorous callings than that of the professional athlete. At left, a mechanic in Washington Heights checks the undercarriage of an automobile; above, a doctor consults with a patient; to the right, a businessman and businesswoman check their computerized inventory. Dominican Americans are eager to avail themselves of educational and economic opportunities that probably would not have been available to them in their homeland.

A Dominican cigar maker in New York City prepares tobacco to be rolled. Hand-rolled Dominican cigars are valued highly by connoisseurs of a fine smoke, particularly in the continued absence of Cuban tobacco products from the American market.

(continued from page 48)

emigrate for political and economic reasons, they have never had to emigrate to escape religious or racial persecution. The Dominican population is composed entirely of the descendants of the Spanish settlers, African slaves, and freedmen, both black and mulatto. Because of extensive intermarriage among these groups, the majority of Dominicans today, are, in varying degrees, of mixed black and white ancestry. In fact, a 1966 census confirmed that 77 percent of the population was mulatto, 12 percent white, and 11 percent black. It is true that attempts to "whiten" the population have been common throughout Dominican history; Trujillo, himself a mulatto, wore white makeup to appear lighter and encouraged European immigration and intermarriage. Nevertheless, education, wealth, and family background—not race—are the primary factors in determining whether or not an individual gains acceptance in society. Religious persecution is virtually nonexistent. The Spanish used the cross as well as the sword to conquer Hispaniola; when Spanish colonists imposed their political institutions on the island's inhabitants, they imposed their religion and language as well. Today, the country is nearly 100 percent Roman Catholic and Spanish speaking. Few, if any, traces of African religion or language remain.

Many American authorities have attempted to classify all Dominican immigrants on the basis of scanty or outdated research. For example, the first and only book dealing exclusively with Dominican immigrants, *The Dominican Diaspora*, by Glenn Hendricks, published in 1974, focused on immigration from Sabana Iglesias, a small village in the agricultural Cibao region in the northern part of the Dominican Republic. The author chose Sabana Iglesias simply as an example of a Dominican village from which many had migrated, but as a result of this focused study, journalists and other students of immigration incorrectly assumed that all Dominicans in the United States were rural peasants, or campesinos. These immigrants were unfairly considered to be unskilled, unfit for certain kinds of work, and prone to unemployment, vice, and reliance on the welfare system.

More recent research, using the results of an extensive survey conducted by the Dominican government in 1974, revealed quite a different picture of the Dominican immigrant. The survey demonstrated that Dominican immigrants are not for the most part rural, poor, and uneducated; in fact, a migrant is much more likely than the average Dominican to be a literate, middle-class, urban dweller. For example, while more than half of the Dominicans who remain behind live in rural areas, only about a quarter of those emigrating come from the countryside. And although only about 60 percent of Dominican nonmigrants can read, nearly all of the migrants surveyed are literate, and 31 percent have had some university education.

The Dominican government's survey also confirmed research done by the INS in the United States that showed that in 1975 about half of the Dominican immigrants were working as professionals, managers, clerical workers, and skilled tradesmen. Immigrants from rural areas would be unlikely to secure such positions. Nevertheless, even though middle-class Dominicans leave their country at the height of their potential productivity because they cannot find employment appropriate to their educational skills, once in America, many are compelled to take jobs for which they are overqualified. Even so, most Dominicans enjoy a better standard of living in the United States than they had at home. Typical is the case of Alilio Perez, an immigrant who studied architecture and engineering at the state university in Santo Domingo. In his country's capital, he lived in a poor *barrio* (neighborhood) and had few clothes or other material possessions. Now living in New York, Perez works as a hairdresser during the day and studies English in the evenings. He finds that his standard of living has improved tremendously, even if his job is not as challenging as the work he was trained to do.

The Dominican immigrants of the 1980s are different from their predecessors in that they are *permanently* fleeing persistent economic disaster—inflation, unemployment, reductions in essential services, heavy foreign debt, and a lack of jobs for skilled workers. In the early 1980s, a Dominican man summed up the people's attitude toward immigration. "If the door were opened to the United States, there would be no one left to close it."

Parents who emigrate hope to provide a better life for their children and to free them from responsibilities more suited to adults. This photo of young Dominican boys at work on a road-building crew was taken in the early 1980s.

Francisco Leo, a Dominican immigrant, runs a small Caribbean restaurant in the Washington Heights section of New York City.

EN NUEVA YORK

"In Santo Domingo," reflected Pedro Escrogima, speaking of the difference between the United States and the Dominican Republic, "you see everybody in the morning and say hello.... In Santo Domingo, you know what the other neighbors are doing because they have their windows open all the time. If something happens over here, you have to wait for the police car. Over there everyone gets involved."

Pedro Escrogima would like to return to the Dominican Republic to live, but he probably will not do so anytime soon. Escrogima came to New York City from the Dominican Republic 20 years ago. A relative helped him to get a job as a presser in the garment industry. Subsequently, he worked as a dishwasher, a busboy, and a doorman. He took English classes at night and, after several years, graduated from Lehman College with a degree in accounting. For a time, Escrogima held an accounting job with the city. He now runs a travel agency in upper Manhattan, providing cheap flights to destinations such as Miami, San Juan, and Santo Domingo for the neighborhood's predominantly Dominican population.

Carmen Fortunato, who has been in the United States since 1977, at first also had trouble adjusting to life in America. Now she is fluent in English and studying at Bronx Community College to be a graphic artist. "It was like being in a jail," she remarks of those early days. "From school to home, that's all I did. I didn't know English and I was afraid because I thought people would laugh when I said something."

New York City, which has a particular attraction for immigrants from the Caribbean and South America, has absorbed perhaps three-quarters of all Dominican immigrants to the United States since the mid-1960s. It is home to the largest community of Dominicans outside Santo Domingo. According to the U.S. Census Bureau, Dominicans constituted the largest group of immigrants to New York City between 1965 and 1980; they were followed by the Jamaicans, the Chinese, and the Haitians. Well over half of the city's Dominicans may be found in northern Manhattan's Washington Heights and Inwood neighborhoods.

Washington Heights

Traditionally, northern Manhattan was divided by the IRT elevated train line that ran along Broadway, with Irish families living on the east side of the street and Jewish families on the west. During the 1950s, Puerto Ricans and Cubans began to move into Washington Heights and Inwood. By the mid-1960s, as the younger Irish and Jewish residents moved out and the older ones died, apartments became available to the Dominicans. Buses crossing the George Washington Bridge to New Jersey allowed the new immigrants easy access to factory jobs as textile workers and domestic positions in private homes. According to Eugenia Georges, assistant professor of anthropology at Rice University, Dominican immigrants found Washington Heights crumbling and full of abandoned buildings and from these modest beginnings built a neighborhood. When the 1980 population census was conducted, Dominicans had largely replaced Irish families on the east side of Broadway.

Today, a visitor who had not seen Washington Heights since 1965 would scarcely recognize it. Vendors sell flowers, bananas, and oranges from stands under the George Washington Bridge. Merengue blasts from sidewalk stereos and from the windows of passing cars. Signs in Spanish advertise a Dominican medical center, a sports club, and a bank. (According to the Dominican Small Business Association, New York houses about 9,000 Dominican businesses.)

But even though the ethnic background of its inhabitants has changed, the neighborhood is still divided. Efrain Frias, of the Northern Manhattan Coalition for Immigrant Rights, says that "from Broadway east, most of the people are Dominicans. On the other side of Broadway, where the houses are better, there are Cubans. . . . I don't know what it is, but at Broadway, there is some kind of invisible wall."

Poverty's Plagues

Although it provides a familiar setting for new Dominican arrivals, Washington Heights is not without its problems. As is much of New York City, Washington Heights is plagued by housing shortages, crime, and drug abuse. Commercial rents have risen, threatening to wipe out many Dominican small businesses, while affordable housing grows more scarce as rental apartments are converted to high-priced cooperatives and condominiums. The drug problem, particularly bad in Washington Heights, has been accompanied by an increase in crime as Dominican youth gangs have become involved in selling drugs. Moses Perez, director of the social service agency Alianza Dominicana (Dominican Alliance), says that many young people fall into drug use because they see so few educational and job opportunities open to them in their neighborhoods.

Although there is some tension between New York City's Puerto Rican and Dominican communities, good relations often prevail. Here, Henry Lopez, a Baptist minister from Puerto Rico, celebrates his installation as minister of a Harlem church with his Dominican wife, Chila.

Dominicans have also settled in Manhattan Valley, a section of Manhattan's upper west side, where they have faced resistance from Puerto Rican families who have been in the neighborhood since the 1950s. In 1981, Josh DeWind, of the Center for Social Sciences at Columbia University, interviewed both Puerto Rican and Dominican residents in Manhattan Valley and uncovered, if not hatred, then the mutual wariness common between an established and a more recently arrived immigrant group. Puerto Rican residents claimed that the Dominicans were taking over the neighborhood and that the Dominicans, because of their intention to return to the Dominican Republic, were unconcerned about keeping the neighborhood clean. Puerto Ricans further accused the Dominicans of not paying their bills and of trying to pass themselves off to immigration authorities as Puerto Rican. The Dominicans in turn charged that the Puerto Ricans were clannish and patronizing and cared only about maintaining political power and achieving their own objectives in the neighborhood.

Other areas of significant Dominican settlement in New York include the Corona section of Queens, Manhattan's Lower East Side, Sunset Park in Brooklyn, and neighborhoods throughout the Bronx. Unfortunately, the Bronx neighborhoods share with Washington Heights the problems of drug abuse and violence.

Dominican Labor in the City

The majority of Dominicans in America, whether documented workers or illegal aliens, perform manual labor. Women work primarily in the garment industry; men do assembly work in small factories or manual work in hospitals, hotels, and restaurants. Some legal residents, and even some undocumented immigrants, hold professional jobs or work as machinists or skilled craftspeople. Documented Dominicans have the advantage over their illegal counterparts in their ability to obtain jobs as sales clerks and to take positions in larger companies. Illegal Dominican workers must take any job at which they can avoid detection. In general, they work longer hours and earn anywhere from 25 to 30 percent less than documented workers. The majority of undocumented Dominicans—particularly women—constitute the workers of a "secondary" labor market composed of small, off-the-books, nonunion manufacturing companies.

Another area in which New York Dominicans have managed to carve out a tiny employment niche is in working for "buckeyes," or hand rollers of cigars, a number of whom are located on Manhattan's Lower West Side. This once active local industry has declined as Americans have cut back on their smoking. Only a third as many cigars were sold in 1987 as were sold in 1964. But of the buckeyes who are still in business, a number are Dominicans, among them Antonio Martinez, the owner of Kenya Hand Made Cigars; Alvis Sanchez; Frank Almanazar; and Jose Pena, who operates Cibao Cigars on West 27th Street.

Martinez, who imports tobacco from the Dominican Republic and other Latin American countries, manufactures about 200 cigars a day. He begins the process of rolling a cigar by gathering tobacco leaves and wrapping them in a single leaf. He then places the cigars into wooden blocks, which are then sealed and placed into a vise for anywhere from a half hour to a whole day in order to press the tobacco together. Finally, Martinez takes the cigars out of the blocks and rolls them in a finishing wrapper. Martinez takes pride in his work. "Anyone can learn how to roll the tobacco. . . . But the difficult part . . . is mixing the tobacco. . . . For each cigar I try to blend different tobacco leaves to create a medium cigar. . . . And, to know the tobacco takes a lifetime."

Hand roller Albert Castellano remembers that "before the Great Depression there were 1,500 cigar manufacturers in New York alone. . . . Some of the larger wholesale factories had 'el lector,' a reader who would sit on a high chair and read newspapers and Cervantes and mystery novels" to the hundreds of cigar rollers, a practice that died with the advent of radio. Other innovations of the 1920s and 1930s—automatic cigar machines and cigarettes—dealt a severe blow to the hand-rolling industry.

Today, the buckeyes face not only declining sales but also Manhattan's exorbitant commercial rents. Still, some continue to hang on, catering to smokers who prefer handmade cigars to those made by machine. Recently, a customer leaving Antonio Martinez's store remarked, "Why shouldn't I support a guy who's trying to make a living here rather than buying from a factory in God knows where?"

Dominican Associations and City Politics

Like other immigrant groups before them, the Dominicans have established a number of mutual benefit organizations. There are about 120 such associations in New York City, including recreational, cultural, civic, and social service groups, each of which tends to attract members on the basis of regional ties, class interests, and family loyalties. The recreational groups help ease the transition to a new country by providing a substitute for the extended family and *compadrazgo*, or "coparenthood," relationships of the homeland; other groups help the Dominican immigrant to achieve a better economic

life in the United States. An example of a civic association devoted to a specific mission is Concilio de Organizaciones Dominicanas (Council of Dominican Organizations), formed in 1972 to fight for the rights of undocumented Dominicans.

Other groups organized to provide social services or achieve political ends include Alianza Dominicana (Dominican Alliance), Asociaciones Dominicanas (Dominican Associations), Asociación Comunal de Dominicanos Progresistas (Community Association of Progressive Dominicans), and the Northern Manhattan Coalition for Immigrant Rights. Among the services these groups offer immigrants are free day care for children, individual and family counseling, and crisis intervention. Classes in English are made available, as are preparation for high school equivalency tests and

In February 1982, Dominicans in New York City held a rally of support at the Cathedral of St. John the Divine for PDR presidential candidate Jorge Salvador Blanco. Partly as the result of maintained close ties to the homeland, Dominicans in the United States have traditionally been more involved in Dominican politics than in American politics.

These signs in Spanish at 163rd Street and Broadway in Manhattan attest to a strong Dominican presence in the neighborhood. In the 1980s, the Dominicans immigrated to New York City at a far faster rate than any other ethnic group.

training in office skills. Dominicans can also obtain immigration-related services at these agencies, such as assistance in filling out government applications.

Perhaps because of the close ties they maintain with the Dominican Republic, Dominican Americans generally remain quite interested in the politics of their home country but avoid political activity in the United States. Julio Hernandez, himself a Dominican immigrant and the Democratic party district leader in Washington Heights, thinks this indifference should change. In 1987, Hernandez commented that "Washington Heights has the highest rate of teen pregnancy in the city, the highest dropout rate, some of the worst housing. I can take you to a five-room apartment where eleven people live." A year and a half later, and with obvious frustration, Hernandez reported that "the majority of the Dominican people are more involved in

Santo Domingo politics than New York.... But I believe they're making a mistake, because if you have a family and kids in New York, you're here. You should fight for what you have here. They do it in reverse."

As have all other new immigrants, Dominicans continue to face mistrust, resentment, and negative stereotyping from those groups already established in America. In the case of Latin American immigrants, these obstacles are reinforced by American prejudices that label Latinos as fun-loving and lazy folk who, try as they might, cannot seem to govern themselves or pay their debts. Miguel Jiminez, a Dominican American living in North Tarrytown, New York, who "came to this country with a dream of the Statue of Liberty," speaks with emotion about his experience, and by extension, of the experience of all other Latin Americans in the United States. "I came to build a better life for myself and my family. But it's not what I thought it would be. There are more closed doors than I ever imagined."

Among the services this storefront office in New York City arranges for Dominicans and other Hispanic immigrants in the community are English classes, legal services, and help with immigration and tax matters. Assistance is provided in both English and Spanish.

A WORLD APART

Perhaps the best known of Dominican cultural traditions is the merengue, the music and dance style that, according to Argentine theater director Hugo Medrano, is "the most authentic expression of the Dominican spirit." In the United States, the sound of merengue from tape players or live bands is one sure sign that the neighborhood has a large Dominican contingent.

The merengue dates back to the birth of the Dominican Republic in 1844, the year in which the country finally gained independence from foreign domination. Originally played with a *tambora* (bass drum) and *güiro* (a dried gourd scraped with a stick), the merengue ensemble, or *perico ripiao*, has come to include an accordion. Around 1915, in the Cibao region of the Dominican Republic, the merengue emerged in its modern form, incorporating aspects of the polka, which had been introduced to the area in the late 19th century.

Although in 1849 the governor of Puerto Rico forbade the dancing of the merengue as scandalous, this uniquely Dominican dance and musical form dominates the contemporary musical scene in Puerto Rico, having replaced the more intricate salsa. Today, the music of many of the more than 200 Dominican merengue groups can be heard, live or on recordings, in cities as far removed from the Dominican Republic as Miami, New York, Caracas, Buenos Aires, and Paris.

Merengue music has flourished both because it has changed with the times and because its light, humorous, and romantic themes have universal appeal. For example, consider the text of a familiar merengue of recent years:

> How pretty is my country.
> There is none other like it.
> It was made by God for us alone.
> This is the only place
> Where the people aren't dumb.
> Where men have principles
> And we are robbed by politicians.

In the experience of the Dominican Americans, dancing the merengue is one of the few cultural traditions that has survived the journey across the ocean intact. Other aspects of traditional Dominican life—particularly the role of women, the organization of the household, and the structure of the family—have been considerably disrupted by immigration.

Dominicans treasure their musical heritage. Each Dominican-American community has its own local bands that keep the sound and spirit of the merengue alive and well in the United States.

A young man in the Dominican Republic in class at a trade school. Many Dominican men in New York find jobs in factories, hospitals, and in the restaurant business; those from urban areas generally fare better than do campesinos with little education or technical training.

Machismo

Dominican society has traditionally been male dominated. Combined with the philosophy of *personalismo*, or personalism, is the Dominican's respect for brave, flamboyant, and macho leaders reminiscent of the caudillos, the strongmen who shaped the country's history. Men from all levels of Dominican society have aspired to this ideal of independent, "manly" behavior. Dictators have ruthlessly repressed political dissent; wealthy men have controlled the distribution of the country's money and land; even peasant farmers with few possessions have been expected to monitor and control the doings of their humble households. In some cases, the desire to emigrate to the United States has provided Dominican men with new opportunities for manipulating Dominican women. A resident of a rural area describes the shameful stratagem used by one of his neighbors who, hoping to emigrate to America, recognized in his daughters a valuable vehicle for his own dreams.

> It used to be that daughters were thought to be largely worthless, because they couldn't work in the fields. But not anymore.... Take the case of José, he was 'blessed' with seven daughters and

one son. It looked like he would have a terrible time maintaining his farm and family. . . . But his daughters are very lovely. . . . I'll tell you, José paraded each one of these daughters dressed to the teeth, and some no older than thirteen, to the young men when they returned [from the United States]. He wouldn't even allow a local boy to look at one of his girls.

Dominican immigrants are likely to be married to other Dominicans. According to a 1982 study, fewer than 40 percent of Dominican immigrants married non-Dominicans, and most of those marriages were to Puerto Ricans. (The children of these mixed marriages were about twice as likely to marry non-Dominicans.) However, the Dominican immigrant men who assume they will run their households in America as dictatorily as they do in the Dominican Republic are often forced to accept a new reality.

Defending the Family

Although wages are higher in the United States than they are in the Dominican Republic, so is the cost of living. Most Dominican-American families find that, far from being able to rely on the income of the husband alone, they can make ends meet only by pooling the income of all family members who can work. This economic reality has dramatically altered the position of Dominican women and the social relations between Dominican husbands and wives. Surveys of recent years indicate that more than half of Dominican immigrant women are in the work force.

Contrary to the impression one might receive from the popular press, not all Dominican women work as sewing-machine operators. A study conducted in the early 1980s found that although about 40 percent of employed Dominican women worked as operatives, another 25 percent held white-collar jobs—as professionals, managers, clerks, or salespeople. With regard to the employers of Dominican women, the study found that about 40 percent of the firms were involved in garment manufacturing but that another 20 percent manufactured other kinds of products; other lines of business accounted for the remaining 40 percent. A resident of Washington Heights confirmed that many people she knew had taken nonmanufacturing jobs, particularly as providers of at-home nursing services to elderly people.

Dominican women have traditionally served as the household's anchor, responsible for the cooking, the domestic chores, and the primary care of the children. Now, in taking on full-time jobs in the United States, Dominican women are earning their own money, which enables them to contribute to the household income and—perhaps more important—to establish more control over their own lives.

No longer can it be said that it is solely up to the Dominican male to "defend the family" economically.

In a sewing shop in El Río, Dominican Republic, local women take part in a UN-sponsored program that teaches them to make shirts and blouses out of sackcloth. A significant percentage of Dominican women in America are employed outside the home, particularly in the garment industry.

Now women believe that they defend the family as well, and they expect to enjoy some of the rights formerly limited to their husbands. Although these women generally say that they work "to help their husbands," they rightly believe that their contribution of a regular income should be met with increased power in making household decisions. Many Dominican immigrant women, when asked to identify the head of their household, now respond, *"los dos"*—"the two of us," husband and wife. One woman commented:

> We are the heads. If both husband and wife are earning salaries then they should equally rule in the household. In the Dominican Republic it is always the husband who gives the orders in the household. But here when the two are working, the woman feels herself equal to the man in ruling the home.

Some women, breaking with established practice and asserting their right to their earnings, refuse to simply turn over their paychecks to their husbands. Instead, they cash the checks themselves and keep a portion for their own use. Some even maintain a separate bank account against their husbands' wishes. To many American women of the late 20th century, this economic independence may not seem revolutionary, but for Dominican women, it is extremely significant. At home in the Dominican Republic, the man spends the family's money for personal luxuries such as rum, cigarettes, and lottery tickets. The woman is only permitted to spend money on goods essential to the household. Her personal needs are often left unmet.

Financial independence, a new sense of self-esteem, and the deep satisfaction of contributing to their children's education have encouraged many Dominican women to make a permanent home in the United States. Many husbands, insecure about their spouses' new self-sufficiency, insist that the family return to the

Many Dominican women in the United States find themselves the sole head of their household. Genoveva (left) is typical of such women. A single mother living in the Boston area, she is studying English in order to improve her family's chances of economic survival.

Dominican Republic. This particular conflict has been the cause of arguments, separation, divorce, and sometimes the return of only part of the family to the homeland.

Unfortunately, not all Dominican immigrant women experience economic and personal liberation. Many still cling to ideas more suited to traditional Dominican society than to life in the United States. "Men are men," they say. "Women are women." A man's proper domain is "the street," and a woman's is "the home." These women believe that men are simply not as well suited to household tasks, such as cooking, cleaning, and raising children. Naturally, Dominican men agree. Although they often demand from their wives an amount of service most Americans would not expect from a paid domestic employee, these men do not believe they need make the smallest effort to help, believing that household work somehow emasculates them or deprives them of their independence.

Many of New York's Dominican immigrant women are separated, divorced, or abandoned by their husbands. These women struggle to maintain a sense of independence and bravely raise their children with help from friends and relatives. Rarely do these single mothers move back in with their extended family. Research in 1981 showed that whereas about half of Dominican households in New York were nuclear-family households (wife, husband, and children), fully 37 percent were single-parent households. Only 12 percent were extended-family households, which might include, for example, grandparents, aunts, and uncles. Not surprisingly, studies have shown that the income of Dominican single-parent households is only about a third of the average for Dominican immigrant families and that close to two-thirds of Dominican single mothers receive some kind of public assistance.

La Familia

The proliferation of single-parent households is evidence of one way in which immigration has altered the Dominican life-style; another related consequence has been the disruption of traditional extended-family networks. This change also has a price that may be expressed in economic terms. In a 1982 article in *Migration Today* about Dominican and Colombian women in New York, Douglas Gurak and Mary Kritz noted that although Colombians fared best financially in a nuclear-family setting, Dominicans fared best in the extended-family household, long a tradition in the Dominican Republic. It is in breaking down these family networks and in forcing Dominicans to develop new modes of economic survival that U.S. immigration policy since 1965, which favors only immediate family members, has grievously failed the Dominican immigrant. Though intended to "unite" families, the policy has in fact had the opposite effect, separating viable, cooperating, close-knit Dominican extended families. The case of the Domínguez family demonstrates the unwitting disruption of such a family unit.

Like many Dominican immigrants, the Domínguez family came from an urban area, and its members were employed in urban occupations. Except for the parents, the family members each had about three to six years of schooling. Mamá bore eight children, but each of her daughters had fewer. Their life in the Dominican Republic, and later on in New York City, was characterized by cooperation and sharing within a family consisting of three generations of siblings and first cousins. In keeping with tradition, the oldest man or woman at any given time had authority over family decisions and welfare, but his or her brothers and sisters were also involved in directing the family's social and financial growth.

María, the first family member to migrate, met a Dominican man, Jorge, in the United States, and they decided to marry. But first María asked Jorge to do her the "favor" of marrying her widowed sister, Rosa, so that Rosa could come to live in the United States. Rosa, in turn, was forced to leave her two children behind in the care of their grandparents until she obtained permanent resident status and could "ask for" them to come to America. At the same time that Jorge and Rosa's *matrimonio de favor* (marriage for favor) was taking place, Jorge asked María to marry his brother so that the brother could enter the United States.

María and Jorge maintained the appearance of their fictional marriages for the benefit of the immigration authorities, even though they were actually living with each other and raising a family. After a few years, Rosa and Jorge ended their "marriage" with a divorce, as did María and Jorge's brother, and María and Jorge made plans to wed legally. But one of their children had been born permanently disabled and required extensive medical care. Jorge and María decided to postpone their legal marriage indefinitely so that the child would be eligible for aid under the Medicaid program, available to María only if she were unmarried. Soon after, Jorge entered into another two-year "marriage for favor" to another cousin.

A few years later, María's cousin Raúl, in the United States illegally after overstaying his tourist visa, fell in love with and married a Dominican woman who already happened to be a permanent resident of the United States. However, because he believed that the woman's family suspected him of marrying *por interés* (just to be eligible to immigrate), Raúl refused to permit his wife to "ask for" him. Raúl returned home and did not come back to the United States until about five years later, when he felt that he had demonstrated his love for his wife, not her citizenship, to her parents.

In 1974, one of María's nieces, Margarita, came to New York for a visit. Margarita was pregnant at the time, and her child was born during the visit, thereby making the child a United States citizen. Margarita and her baby soon returned to the Dominican Republic. At around the same time, Margarita's aunt Virginia had given birth to a baby in the Dominican Republic. Unfortunately, the child suffered from colic, diarrhea, vomiting, and anemia. Seeing an opportunity to obtain better medical care for his daughter's child, Virginia's father borrowed Margarita's child's papers and used them to bring Virginia's child into the United States.

The story of the Domínguez family illustrates the range of legal and illegal mechanisms that Dominicans have developed to help reunite and support their families. Common schemes include arranging for a job in the United States from the Dominican Republic; having a relative "ask for" another relative; marrying for favor; overstaying a tourist visa; borrowing papers; arranging a marriage that is strictly a *matrimonio de negocio*, or business transaction; and renting the passport of a United States citizen or permanent resident. In discussing various immigration options, the Domínguez family made it clear that they found unacceptable the alternatives of crossing borders without any papers or of deceiving a U.S. permanent resident or citizen by proposing marriage under false pretenses, *por interés*.

Nevertheless, for this Dominican family, as for many others, immigration regulations do not prevent entry. The regulations merely cause delays, as well as stress and strain on family relationships. Ironically, the relationships most disrupted are those that U.S. immigration law is supposed to protect—bonds between spouses and those between parents and their children. Legally married couples often find it advantageous to divorce each other, and people already living together may be unable to marry because they are part of marriages for business or favor. Parents are often separated from their children, and because American legal definitions of kinship relations are often at variance with Dominican definitions, the children born to parents of a "free union," who may both be legally married to

Young Dominicans in costumes march in a Dominican parade in Washington Heights, New York. As more Dominicans choose to make their home in America and come to enjoy the economic and social benefits of U.S. citizenship, their children are sure to prosper from a greater sense of cultural stability.

A WORLD APART

Dominican cultural life in America includes participation in local parades celebrating Dominican dance, music, and national pride. This Dominican woman offers a basket of food representing the fertility of her homeland.

others, bear questionable U.S. legal status, as well as the psychological burden of secrecy.

It is clear from the experience of the Domínguez family that America's current immigration policy does not always foster the unity and solidarity of immigrant families. The law now emphasizes the bringing together of spouses and the uniting of parents with their young children. A more comprehensive immigration policy would recognize that important bonds also exist between brothers and sisters, between children and their aunts or uncles, and between parents and their adult children. It would reduce the need for illegal mechanisms, the number of illegal aliens, and a great deal of stress that now exists in the Dominican community.

Nevertheless, in spite of the strain of subterfuge and separation, members of the Domínguez clan insist that New York City has been for them "the best place to get ahead, or to improve your life," although they do add that "the Dominican Republic is the best place to be if you are down and out or have problems." The family is happy for the opportunity that immigration has brought. When the relatives gather for dinner, Raúl says in Spanish, "Anyone who is hungry here, raise your hand." Then, when no one raises a hand, Raúl says—in English—"God Bless America!"

Although baseball was introduced in the Dominican Republic in the early 20th century, it was not until the late 1950s that Dominican players found fame in America. Since then, the Dominican government has built 3 professional baseball stadiums; the town of San Pedro alone has about 200 teams. For many Dominican youths, a career in major league baseball is truly "the American dream."

BASEBALL— CHASING THE DREAM

Ask an American sports fan what comes to mind when you say "Dominican," and the chances are good that he or she will answer, "Baseball."

Dominican immigrants have enjoyed their most conspicuous public success to date in baseball. The St. Louis Cardinal power-hitting first baseman Pedro Guerrero, the Toronto Blue Jays' slugger George Bell, and former Cardinal pitcher Joaquín Andújar are just 3 of the dozens of major league ballplayers to come out of the Dominican Republic in the last 20 years. Many of these players have come from San Pedro de Macorís, a sugar-producing port city of about 125,000. Guerrero, Bell, and Andújar aside, San Pedro is most celebrated for its production of players with the right combination of skills—agility, range, fielding ability, and a strong throwing arm—to play the demanding position of *mediocampista*, or shortstop. Toronto's Tony Fernandez,

Young fans watch a baseball game in the Dominican city of San Pedro de Macorís, where the allure of baseball cuts across all social and economic lines. For the children of poor sugar-mill workers, baseball can seem like a magic solution to poverty and obscurity.

arguably the best shortstop in baseball, Rafael Santana of the Cleveland Indians, Alfredo Griffin of the Los Angeles Dodgers, and Julio Franco of the Texas Rangers (Franco began his career as a shortstop but now plays second base) are idols in San Pedro, their relatively luxurious off-season homes the subject of informal tours led by poor children hoping to earn a few pennies.

No one knows why San Pedro produces baseball players in such astonishing quantities, but it is probably due in part to historical accident. Around the turn of the century, American businessmen came to the Dominican Republic to take advantage of the rich sugar-producing land around San Pedro, a town that lies along the Dominican Republic's south coast, about 40 miles east of Santo Domingo. Before long, San Pedro became a sugar-mill town, and the American owners of the mills sponsored local contests for company baseball teams. The mill workers, accustomed to the backbreaking work of cutting sugarcane with machetes, had developed strength and stamina, qualities that would help make them excellent baseball players. As the years passed, local rivalries between teams intensified. During the U.S. occupation (1916–24), baseball became even more firmly rooted in the Dominican Republic.

It was not until the late 1950s and early 1960s, however, that Dominican baseball players found success in the United States. Ozzie Virgil, pitching legend Juan Marichal (inducted into the Baseball Hall of Fame in 1983), Felipe Alou and his brothers Matty and Jesus were all signed by the Giants, while Rico Carty, the first Macorista (San Pedro de Macorís resident) to achieve long-term success, was signed by the Milwaukee Braves. The achievement of these men prompted the Dominican government to build 3 professional baseball stadiums, including 1 in San Pedro, and by 1985, this baseball-crazy town was drawing young people from all over the island to play on its 200 teams.

Manito

More than any other Dominican ballplayer of the early years, pitcher Juan Marichal set the standards of excellence that future Dominican players have sought to measure up to. Marichal was born in Laguna Verde in 1938 in a palm-bark shack inhabited by his extremely poor farming family. Marichal's father died when his son was only three years old, and the boy known as Manito was raised by his mother and older brother, Gonzalo. Marichal quit high school after the 11th grade to play baseball, first as an amateur for Monte Cristi, the United Fruit Company, and the Dominican air force, and then professionally for the Escogido Leones. In 1958, the San Francisco Giants gave him a $500 signing bonus; Marichal pitched for several minor league teams in the United States before joining the Giants during the 1960 season.

Marichal's chubby face and mischievous smile earned him the nicknames Laughing Boy and the Dominican Dandy, but on the mound he was serious and determined. In his first major league game, Marichal pitched a one-hit shutout against the Philadelphia Phillies. Physically intimidating at 6 feet tall and 185 pounds, Marichal had a dramatic, high-kicking windup and a varied delivery that kept opposing batters consistently off balance. From 1963 to 1969, Marichal won more games than any other pitcher in baseball, and he led the National League in various pitching categories year after year. Known for his amazing control, Marichal won 243 games during his 16-year major league career, twice helped the Giants to first-place finishes, and was named to play in the All-Star Game 8 times.

Despite his undeniable greatness as a hurler, Marichal never received baseball's Cy Young Award, given annually to the best pitcher in each league. This was because in each of Marichal's greatest years, another pitcher was even more spectacular. In 1963, Marichal led the National League with 25 wins and 321 innings pitched, but the legendary southpaw of the Los Angeles Dodgers, Sandy Koufax, matched his victory total and topped the senior circuit in shutouts, strikeouts, and earned run average. Five years later, Marichal again led the league in victories, this time with 26 (20 wins is the standard mark of excellence), but that year Bob Gibson, the fiercely competitive right-hander of the St. Louis Cardinals, set an all-time mark for lowest earned run average and walked off with the award. Marichal's long-term achievements, however, proved impossible to overlook. In 1983, Marichal became the first Latin American admitted to the Baseball Hall of Fame under the normal selection process. (Roberto Clemente, a native of Puerto Rico who for 18 years was a brilliant right fielder for the Pittsburgh Pirates, was admitted by a special vote soon after his untimely death in 1972.) Family members have carried on Marichal's legacy of achievement; his son-in-law, José Rijo, also a Dominican, is an outstanding pitcher for the Cincinnati Reds.

Displaying his trademark high kick, Juan Marichal delivers a pitch against the Los Angeles Dodgers on September 20, 1969. Marichal's win that day was his 20th of the season.

Marichal's stellar career, which ended in 1975, was marred by one unfortunate incident. During a crucial game in the summer of 1965 with the Dodgers, who traditionally have been the Giants' fiercest rivals, the generally good-natured and cheerful Marichal initiated a wild melee when he clubbed Dodger catcher John Roseboro over the head with a bat. The attack followed a pitch from Koufax that almost hit Marichal, who also objected to Roseboro's return throw zinging past his ear. Marichal was suspended for 9 days and fined $1,750 for his part in the fracas. Fortunately, Roseboro was not seriously injured, but the outburst contributed to the stereotype that still persists about Latin American ballplayers—that they are high-strung, moody, temperamental, and prone to volcanic eruptions of anger.

One Tough Dominican

In the 1980s, this stereotype was lent further credence because of the antics of Joaquín Andújar, the self-proclaimed "one tough Dominican," who enjoyed his greatest success as a pitcher with the St. Louis Cardinals, one of the decade's most successful franchises. Although Andújar helped the Cardinals reach the World Series twice and won first 20 and then 21 games in the 1984 and 1985 seasons, he was as notorious for his unpredictable behavior as he was celebrated for his performances on the mound. In the seventh and decid-

Andújar (right, pointing) forcibly debates a call in the seventh game of the 1985 World Series. His vociferous objections led to his being ejected from the contest.

ing game of the 1982 World Series, Andújar, near completion of a sterling outing, was practically carried off the field by his teammates after a heated argument with some Milwaukee players. The Milwaukee players later admitted that they were well aware of Andújar's notorious temper and had taunted him with the intention of goading him into an outburst. In the seventh game of the 1985 World Series, with the Cardinals trailing 9–0, Andújar bumped and threatened an umpire so viciously that he was thrown out of the game and suspended for the first 10 days of the 1986 season. This incident occurred at a time when major league baseball was trying to solve its drug problem, and Andújar, suspected of drug use, was ordered by the commissioner of baseball to contribute $115,000 to a drug prevention program, perform community service, and submit to drug testing.

Andújar's tantrums consistently overshadowed his impressive pitching accomplishments. He frequently complained that the news media had him pegged as a troublemaker and ignored any attempts he made to improve his image. In a 1985 interview with *Sport* magazine, he said: "If you go to the 7-Eleven to buy a magazine, you have to look a long time before you find my name. Every time they write about Joaquín, it's something bad. I saw my picture in *The Sporting News*. They don't even mention my name. They just show a picture of me and Ozzie Virgil fighting. Why do they do that? I'm not the only guy who fights in the stadium. They just want to make Joaquín look like a clown or stupid."

Andújar's criticism of the news media was part of his general belief that he was treated unfairly by the baseball world—not being awarded the Player of the Week and Player of the Year honors he thought he deserved, being passed over as the starting pitcher for the 1985 All-Star Game, doing poorly in the voting for the prestigious Cy Young Award, not being asked to conduct baseball skills "clinics" for young American prospects. Although he refused to say so in public, it was clear that Andújar believed that Latin American players were treated with less respect than were North American players due to the cultural differences and racial prejudices of sportswriters and fans.

Responding, for example, to the charge that he occasionally threw pitches that were meant to either hit or intimidate batters, Andújar argued that Dominican pitchers were being held to a higher standard than were American pitchers: "The hitters want the room service right down the middle. They want me to prepare the food, take it to their room, spoon it into their mouths and eat it. . . . Steve Carlton [an extremely successful white American pitcher] pitches inside. I don't see anybody fighting with Steve Carlton. . . . But when Joaquín Andújar or Mario Soto [then Cincinnati Red pitcher and Dominican Republic native] pitches inside, everybody goes out to the mound to fight. If they want to fight . . . they should go to the Middle East. I just want to play baseball."

In 1986, the Cardinals traded Andújar to the Oakland Athletics, a move that was both praised by Cardinal fans (by those who said Andújar was washed up as a pitcher and was too hard to manage) and criticized (by those who pointed at Joaquín's back-to-back 20-win seasons). None of his critics, however, could question Andújar's devotion to the game. For example, he always talked in terms of pitching complete (nine-inning) games, a practice that in recent years has become somewhat obsolete. When he was with the Cardinals, Joaquín averaged an amazing eight innings per outing for four straight years, from 1982 to 1985. Shortly after the trade to Oakland, Joaquín told the Athletics' hot young pitching prospect at the time, 20-year-old José Rijo (for whom Andújar was something of a role model) that a pitcher who didn't want to pitch a full 9 innings had "no guts."

If Andújar seemed to be more tranquil and at home in his first season with the Athletics, there were several good reasons. The Athletics' team leader was Dominican shortstop Alfredo Griffin, Andújar's next-door neighbor back home in Santo Domingo. And the Athletics' director of scouting for Latin America and a troubleshooting pitching coach for the organization was none other than Manito himself: Andújar's boyhood idol, Juan Marichal. Unfortunately, arm troubles prevented Andújar from duplicating his previous success.

Getting Off the Island

Two other Dominican baseball stars of the 1980s, Mario Soto and George Bell, have had careers similar to Andújar's in that their considerable athletic achievements were sometimes overshadowed by their temperamental outbursts. Soto's talent was so immense that he was dubbed "the next Juan Marichal," and he was one of baseball's best pitchers during the mid-1980s. Bell, a hard-hitting left fielder for the Toronto Blue Jays, received the American League's Most Valuable Player Award in 1987. But Soto's explosions of rage were downright frightening and sometimes dangerous, and Bell's feuds with managers and fans have led to his being depicted as a sullen, selfish ballplayer.

Soto grew up in Baní, a city of about 40,000 to the southwest of Santo Domingo. His first home was just a tiny two-room shack, without plumbing or electricity, located near the hot sugarcane fields. His father left the family when Mario was eight, and the young boy helped his mother, Marta, who took in laundry for the Dominican marines. Although Soto's brother and sister moved out when they became older, Mario continued to live at home. At the age of 15, he quit school—which he had enjoyed—to work as a mason for a local contractor. At first, Mario earned only $1.50 for 12 hours of work, but he eventually worked his way up to $7.50 a day. No matter how much money he earned, he always gave half of it to his mother.

Soto started playing baseball as a teenager, and the Cincinnati Reds, impressed with his pitching, signed him for $1,000. After several years in the minor leagues, in 1980 Soto joined the Reds. Before long he became known for his excellent pitching ability—and for a tendency to become rattled when umpires made calls with which he disagreed or when fans heckled him. In 1983, Soto turned in one excellent performance after another, but the Reds were unable to score runs for him and Soto lost nearly as many games as he won. He reacted by exerting even more pressure on himself to perform flawlessly. Surprisingly, the financial security offered by a lucrative multiyear contract he signed in 1984 had the same sobering effect on Soto, who felt obliged to give a perfect performance in return for his huge paychecks. "As long as I feel that they didn't waste their money, that's the only thing I'm worried about," he said.

Soto shared Andújar's belief that being Latin American—particularly Dominican—put him at an automatic disadvantage with respect to popularity, both with the fans and the news media. In 1984, he was quoted as saying that "people in Cincinnati are just jealous because of all the great players they've had. I happened to get the best contract—and they cannot take that, a guy coming from the Dominican Republic. They cannot *take* that." (Soto's contract made him the highest-paid player in the history of the ball club.) Again like Andújar, Soto believes that writers are only interested in covering Dominican players when they are in trouble. Said Soto of his superb first half of the 1984 season (which was followed by two five-day suspensions for fighting), "I was pitching *great*, and nobody came to talk to me. I've been to the All-Star Game three straight years, and nobody talks about that. Then, when this trouble starts, everybody comes and talks."

The trouble Soto alluded to certainly did provoke conversation among sports aficionados. It also cost Soto over $6,000 in fines as well as playing time lost to suspension. In the first incident, Soto charged out of the dugout at an umpire and had to be tackled and held by

In this game in September 1985, Cincinnati Red pitcher Mario Soto recorded 14 strikeouts against the San Francisco Giants but still lost. One of baseball's most talented pitchers in his prime, Soto displayed a limited capacity to deal with the game's frustrations.

Red catcher Brad Gulden, manager Vern Rapp, and Chicago Cub coach Don Zimmer. As he was being led off the field, a food vendor threw a cup of ice at Soto, prompting him to grab a bat and attempt to jump into the stands in pursuit of the vendor.

The second incident was more serious. In a game in Atlanta, Soto threw a pitch close to batter Claudell Washington. Washington ran out to the pitcher's mound and got into a scuffle with Soto. Then, after Washington had been wrestled to the ground, Soto reared back and, from only a few feet away, threw his best fastball directly at Washington's head. Fortunately, the pitch was wild, or Washington could have been seriously injured and Soto might have been banned from baseball for good. Shortly after that brawl, Soto foully insulted local sportswriter Lonnie Wheeler (who had merely written a factual account of the fight), then twice taunted Wheeler in a confrontation at the ballpark: "When you going to stop writing these stories? When somebody breaks your neck?"

Mario Soto is a proud man who, as a teenager, endured tremendous hardship and poverty in trying to support his family. It is obvious that he has never forgotten those years. "When I was growing up," he told an interviewer, "that's when I really needed help, and nobody helped me. When my mother barely made enough money for us to get something to eat, nobody came up to me and say, 'What's your problem?' Nobody say I have a temper. Now everybody say I have a temper. They don't know nothing about me. I don't need their help."

Although Soto bought a home in a middle-class Cincinnati suburb and perfected his English, picking up something of a California accent, he remains very much a Dominican. Even after his marriage, Soto returned to Santo Domingo every year during the off-season to live in a house he shared with his mother. Eight years after coming to the United States, and earning nearly $1 million a year, he still frets about upholding the Dominican tradition that mandates that a man must "defend the household." Soto says that his wife does not work—"I make enough money to take care of my family." In explaining his almost homicidal behavior in the Atlanta fight, Soto displayed his preoccupation with protecting his family and home—"If you have family and someone attacks you and you run away, how you gonna explain that?"—and then made a comparison that did not satisfy many of his listeners. "What would you do," asks Soto, "if someone came into your house and attacked you? Wouldn't you fight back?" Mario Soto is not the only Dominican player who feels that the American journalists and fans fail to understand him. In 1987, the year he won the coveted American League Most Valuable Player Award, the Toronto Blue Jays superstar George Bell told those gathered at the annual dinner of the New York Baseball Writers: "A lot of people, they don't know who George Bell is.... Find out who I am, and we get along pretty good!"

Born in Ingenio Santa Fe, a small sugar-mill town just north of San Pedro, George Bell, the oldest of five children, started out with very little. The neighborhood was no more than a cluster of rude wooden shanties, each with a corrugated-tin roof and two or three dark

In 1987, George Bell of the Toronto Blue Jays won the American League's Most Valuable Player Award. Bell credits his father with instilling in him a sense of purpose and pride. Bell often shares his wealth and expertise with the children of Santo Domingo.

rooms for an entire family. As in Mario Soto's childhood home, there was no running water, and the smell of sugar being refined was inescapable. If it were not for his splendid athletic abilities and his father's encouragement, Bell would probably have ended up like most of his neighbors, working at a $2,000-a-year sugar-mill job. Bell's father, George, who drove a sugarcane train out of San Pedro, sometimes taking his oldest son along for the ride, instilled a fighting spirit in his children. According to the younger Bell, he "made us aggressive in everything . . . told us we had to fight for what we thought."

In 1978, the Philadelphia Phillies signed the 18-year-old Bell for $3,500. Although he had been playing baseball for 10 years, Bell was required to spend a few years in the minor leagues. The Phillies sent him to Helena, Montana, where, as a Spanish-speaking black from a Caribbean island, he met with ridicule and suspicion from both local people and players. Reflecting on the experience in 1988, Bell admitted that "it very hard for you in new country. Nobody like you. The other players, they look down on Latin players. Black, white, no matter, they don't trust anybody who speak Spanish. If you Latin American, they say,'You crazy.' If you Latin American, they say, 'You steal.' My first year terrible. It hurt a lot."

Even after being picked up by the Blue Jays in 1980, recognition was a long time coming for George Bell. From 1984 to 1987, his first four seasons in the major leagues, Bell put up better and better statistics each year. Nevertheless, he went largely unnoticed, losing out in the Toronto sportswriters' Player of the Year voting and in the Toronto fans' voting for players to participate in baseball's annual All-Star Game.

To a great extent, the lack of media attention was a result of Bell's reluctance to talk to the press. Bell experienced great difficulty with English, and this difficulty created unfortunate misunderstandings; writers often got the impression that Bell was rude or arrogant.

With charming honesty, Bell once told an interviewer, "I no understand [why] if newspapers want story about me they no get translator. That's be treat people nice." Indeed, having a translator might have helped Bell avoid much of the bad press he received about his flamboyant playing style and uncompromising approach to the game.

In 1987, Bell signed a contract that would pay him about $2 million annually for the next 2 years. Although Bell's offensive production has dropped somewhat in recent years (his league-leading 47 home runs and 134 runs batted in for 1987 were hard totals to match), he continues to be San Pedro de Macorís's brightest star. Each winter Bell returns to San Pedro, where he has 2 off-season homes, 1 of which is a $450-a-day villa at the luxury beach resort Casa de Campo. In spite of his wealth, however, Bell is conscious of his country's poverty and donates tens of thousands of dollars to medical care for Dominican children, brings truckloads of baseball equipment to San Pedro, and spends his days working out with and coaching Dominican players from the Houston Astros' minor league teams. Bell admits that he likes teaching baseball skills to young people, but says, "Three things I teach more. . . . Be tough. Be winner. Be nice person. Those are three main things in life."

For all the publicity surrounding colorful star players like Andújar, Soto, and Bell, Dominican immigrants have made their biggest contribution to baseball as shortstops—known in Spanish as *mediocampistas* or *campocortistas*. On one day in April 1986, no fewer than nine Dominicans played shortstop for U.S. major league baseball teams. Among the more well known players in that group were Tony Fernandez of the Toronto Blue Jays, Rafael Santana, then of the New York Mets, Alfredo Griffin of the Oakland Athletics (now a Los Angeles Dodger), Julio Franco of the Cleveland Indians (now a Texas Ranger), and José Uribe of the San Francisco Giants. So many Dominicans have made it to big league

Toronto Blue Jays shortstop Tony Fernandez leaps over Johnny Ray of the California Angels during an unsuccessful double-play attempt. As do many Dominican ballplayers, Fernandez makes his off-season home on the island.

teams as shortstops that only a true baseball fan could chronicle a complete list of names and teams. But one man in particular stands out both in hitting and in fielding: Tony Fernandez.

Fernandez grew up in San Pedro de Macorís. He and his family lived in a simple cement house so close to the city's Tetelo Vargas Stadium that a home run by Pittsburgh Pirates catcher Tony Peña once bounced off its wall. A small boy with a bad knee, Cabeza (Head), as he was known because of his large cranium, practiced his fielding skills while doing odd jobs at the stadium. Aided by a knee operation and natural ability, Fernandez eventually obtained a contract with the Toronto Blue Jays and in 1985 became their full-time shortstop. A graceful, quick fielder, perhaps the best at his position in the big leagues, Fernandez is also an excellent hitter and a canny base runner. He has been so valuable to his team that many people believe that a knee injury that sidelined him in the closing days of the 1987 season cost Toronto the pennant that year. Much of Fernandez's off-season time is spent performing missionary work as a Pentecostal Christian in Santo Domingo, where he makes his off-season home with his wife and son.

In 1985, at least 71 Dominican shortstops were under contract to major league teams. Perhaps part of the reason Dominicans play the position so well is that they are generally of a small build and so are able to move quickly and agilely. Some Dominicans have speculated that the poor conditions under which they learned the game have contributed to their success. After playing the game on rocky fields, with gloves made from old milk cartons, balls made from sewed-up socks, bats made from guava-tree limbs, playing the game on smooth grass (or artificial turf) with expensive equipment seems easy by comparison.

Indeed, the entrenched poverty that is the lot of so many Dominicans does much to explain their spectacular success in baseball. For many young Dominican men, baseball represents their only real prospect for success. Many may never have known someone who went to college and achieved professional success, but most have heard of George Bell, Tony Fernandez, and Juan Marichal, of their athletic triumphs in los Estados Unidos (the United States), and of the wealth they have earned. The impoverished background of many Dominican baseball players helps explain everything from their batting style to the ferocity with which Dominicans react when they perceive that the prize that they have obtained through so much hard work— their athletic success—is in some way endangered. (Dominican players are usually aggressive, slashing hitters fond of swinging at any pitch near the plate; for that reason they rarely draw walks. The more classic approach calls for a hitter to concentrate on pitches within the strike zone; Dominicans are, in baseball parlance, notorious "bad-ball hitters." Rafael Ramírez, a veteran major league shortstop from the Dominican Republic, explained this predilection by saying, "You can't walk off the island." In other words, it is base hits, and not walks, that attract the attention of the major league scouts who reward talented young players with contracts to play in the United States.) It is interesting to note that the same reasons—impoverished economic background, the relative denial of other avenues of success, the prevalence of athletes as role models—have been given to explain the outstanding achievement of black athletes in the United States. As is true of Dominicans in professional baseball, black athletes in the United States have attained a level of success far greater than their numbers in society would have indicated. Black athletes have also been assigned the same stigmas as have Dominican ballplayers—they are said to be moody, temperamental, and difficult to manage and coach. Like black athletes, Dominican ballplayers have rarely received credit for the tremendous amount of self-discipline and hard work that has enabled them to exercise such athletic prowess. (The reader should also be aware, if it is not already self-evident, that not all Dominican ballplayers are brawlers on the diamond and that players of all races have been known to engage in fisticuffs and related mayhem and mischief. Indeed, some of the national pastime's most rowdy episodes occurred while it was still strictly segregated.)

The success of Dominicans as baseball players in the United States is one of the most colorful and improbable of immigrant success stories. Unfortunately, it represents success for only a tiny portion of the thousands of Dominicans who come to the United States every year in hopes of improving their economic status. In the Dominican Republic, competition for contracts with major league organizations is keen. For every George Bell or Tony Fernandez, there are dozens of Dominican boys who never catch the eye of a big league scout. And with the poor quality of education and lack of economic opportunity in towns like San Pedro, the only alternatives for these young men are low-paying jobs in skilled trades, the sugar-refining industry (now in decline), or light manufacturing. Perhaps that is why Toronto Blue Jays scout Epy Guerrero shouted what he did to a group of infielders about to head north to minor league teams: "*¡Tú eres el hombre de la Mancha, cazando el sueño!*" "You are Don Quixote, chasing the dream!"

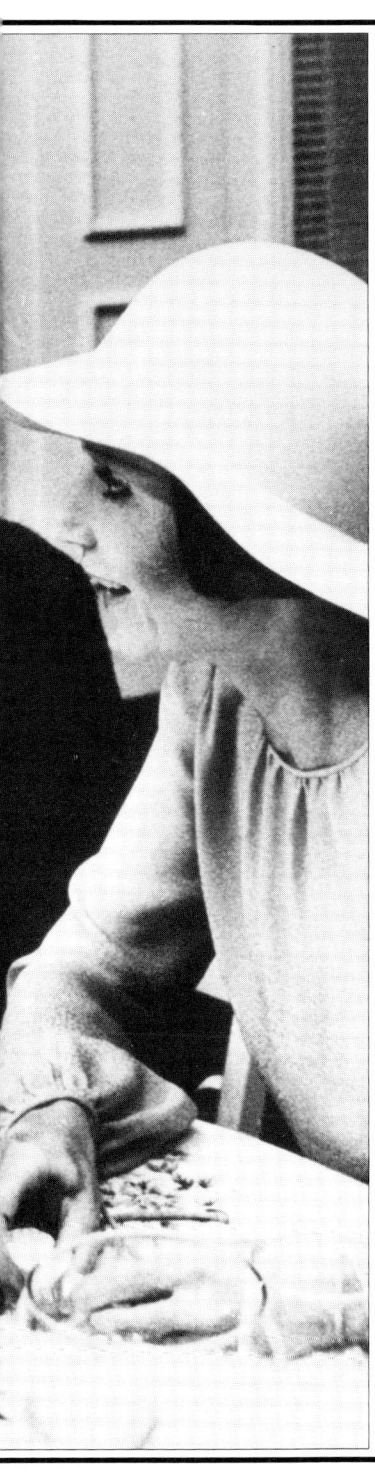

Fashion designer Oscar de la Renta, shown here in 1977 with Susan Mary Alsop (left) and Mary McFadden (right), is perhaps the most well known Dominican outside the sports world. In 1982, de la Renta founded La Casa del Niño, *or* The Home of the Child, *a nonprofit institution in La Romana dedicated to providing education and health care to needy children.*

ON TO THE SECOND GENERATION

Dominican migration is a relatively recent phenomenon. Dominicans have been coming to America in significant numbers only since 1961, and for many years, particularly from 1966 to 1978, most emigrants had no intentions of establishing a permanent home in the United States. But when the Dominican Republic's economy collapsed in the early 1980s, emigration grew more popular, and most emigrants were compelled to consider the possibility of a more permanent stay in, or of more frequent visits to, America. According to Frank Moya Pons, professor of history at Columbia University, a large number of the Dominicans who had repatriated in the 1970s were forced to return to the United States throughout the 1980s in a quest for steady work and a decent wage.

While a few talented Dominican immigrants have made their fortunes as baseball players, the majority have made only a modest living in less than luxurious surroundings. Aside from sports figures, perhaps the only other Dominican known to the American and European public is the fashion designer Oscar de la Renta.

But as a more recent immigrant group than either the Puerto Ricans or the Cubans, to whom they are sometimes compared, the Dominicans cannot be judged harshly for not yet having achieved what these other groups have achieved. Several practical circumstances besides their newness set them apart from other Hispanic groups in the United States. Puerto Ricans are born U.S. citizens; Dominicans must be permanent residents in the United States for five years before they can apply for citizenship. It is not surprising that Puerto Ricans, who have in the past constituted 80 percent of the Hispanics in New York City eligible to vote, have been able to obtain and to hold considerable political power there. As more Dominicans—perhaps a third of New York City's Hispanics—become legalized under the 1986 Immigration Reform and Control Act, which grants amnesty to illegal aliens who have been in the United States since 1982, and as these newly legalized permanent residents go on to apply for U.S. citizenship, Dominicans could play a significant role in the New York City mayoral elections in 1993 and 1997.

The economic success of the Cubans in the United States has a rather unique explanation. During and after the Communist revolution of 1958–59, as a result of which Fidel Castro took power, the wealthy associates of Cuba's former dictator, fearing reprisal for their political associations and confiscation of their property, fled to the United States. These and others with "political refugee" status settled mainly in Miami and New York City, where they put their money to work. Today, the Cuban Americans wield considerable economic power in both of these cities. The majority of Dominicans who have left their country for political and economic reasons, however, have been lower-to-middle-class city dwellers—certainly not individuals with

ready money to invest in new business ventures. In addition, annual visits to the Dominican Republic and the rapid growth of a native Spanish-speaking population in urban areas of the Northeast have slowed the Dominicans' acculturation into mainstream, English-speaking American society.

The Dominican influx shows no sign of abating. It is unlikely that the Dominican Republic's economy will be rebuilt anytime soon, and the huge Dominican presence in the United States makes immigration, even for part of each year, ever more attractive. And because the methods of illegal immigration grow more refined every day, immigration authorities and legislators can at best hope to slow down, not to dam, this human flood.

In February 1990, the 12th annual Carnaval de Merengue *played to a capacity crowd at New York City's Madison Square Garden. As the Dominican population in the United States continues to grow, Dominican culture is likely to exert an ever greater influence.*

FURTHER READING

Black, Jan Knippers. *The Dominican Republic: Politics and Development in an Unsovereign State.* Boston: Allen and Unwin, 1986.

Bray, David. "Economic Development: The Middle Class and International Migration in the Dominican Republic." *International Migration Review* 18 (2): 217–36 (1984).

Chaney, Elsa M., and Constance R. Sutton, eds. *Caribbean Life in New York City: Sociocultural Dimensions.* New York: Center for Migration Studies, 1987.

Diederich, Bernard. *Trujillo: The Death of the Goat.* Boston: Little, Brown, 1978.

Foner, Nancy, ed. *New Immigrants in New York.* New York: Columbia University Press, 1987.

Gleijeses, Piero. *The Dominican Crisis: The 1965 Constitutionalist Revolt and American Intervention.* Baltimore: The Johns Hopkins University Press, 1978.

Hendricks, Glenn. *The Dominican Diaspora: From the Dominican Republic to New York City—Villagers in Transition.* New York: Teachers College Press, 1974.

Wiarda, Howard J. *The Dominican Republic: Nation in Transition.* New York: Praeger, 1969.

INDEX

Africans, 24, 57
Agua Santa del Yuna, 42
Alianza Dominicana (Dominican Alliance), 63, 67
Andújar, Joaquín, 85, 90–93
Asociación Comunal de Dominicanos Progresistas (Community Association of Progressive Dominicans), 67
Asociaciones Dominicanas (Dominican Associations), 67

Badillo, Herman, 18
Báez, Buenaventura, 27, 28
Balaguer, Joaquín, 19, 33–35
Baní, Dominican Republic, 93
Barrio, 59
Baseball, 85–103
Baseball Hall of Fame, 87, 88
Bell, George, 85, 93, 96–99
Benefactor, el. See Trujillo, Generalissimo Rafael Leónidas
Blanco, Salvador Jorge, 34
Border Patrol, U.S., 45
Bosch, Juan, 19, 33
Bronx, New York, 64
Bronx Community College, 62
Brooklyn, New York, 64
Buenos Aires, Argentina, 72

Cabral, Eugenio, 43, 44
Cáceres, Alfredo, 38–40
Cáceres, Ramon, 27
Camacho, Ramon Emilio Santana, 39, 40, 42
Campesinos, 58
Caracas, Venezuela, 72
Caribbean Sea, 14, 24, 37, 62
Casa de Campo, Dominican Republic, 99
Castro, Fidel, 17, 106

Caudillos, 73
Cédula, 47
Census Bureau, U.S., 62
Center for Social Sciences, 64
Central Intelligence Agency (CIA), 14, 33
Chinese, 62
Cibao, 58
"Cibaoen in New York, A," 19
Ciudad Trujillo, Dominican Republic, 13
Columbians, 78
Columbia University, 64, 105
Columbus, Bartholomeo, 22
Columbus, Christopher, 21–23
Compadrazgo, 66
Concilio de Organizaciones Dominicanas (Council of Dominican Organizations), 67
Conquistadores, 22
Corona, Queens, 16, 64
Corredor. See Visa broker
Cuba, 15, 106
Cubans, 15, 17, 44, 62, 63, 106
Cy Young Award, 88, 91

Death's Head Beach, 43
Democratic party, 68
Department of Natural Resources (Puerto Rico), 42
Dominican Americans
　description of average immigrant, 57, 58
　family relationships, 78–83
　gender roles in the United States, 73–78
　hazards of illegal immigration, 43, 44
　living conditions in U.S. cities, 63, 64
　methods of illegal immigration to United States, 37–45

methods of legal immigration to United States, 46–48
musical traditions, 71, 72
participation in baseball, 85–103
political associations, 67
population in Puerto Rico, 41
population in the United States, 16, 62
reasons for emigration, 30–35
route taken by immigrants to the United States, 41, 42
stereotypes, 58
and U.S. immigration policy, 17, 18
Dominican Diaspora, The (Hendricks), 57
Dominican Revolutionary party (PDR), 19, 32–34
Dominican Small Business Association, 63

El Paso, Texas, 41
England, 27
Escrogima, Pedro, 61

Fair of Peace and Fraternity of the Free World, 14
Fernandez, Tony, 85, 100, 101
Flores, Augustin Genal, 38–40
Flores, Rafael, 38–40
Flores, Veridiana, 39
Florida, 21, 37, 44
Fortunato, Carmen, 62
France, 24, 25, 27
French, 24, 25
French Revolution, 25

George Washington Bridge, 62, 63
Guerrero, Pedro, 85

Haiti, 15, 18, 21, 25, 26
Haitians, 44, 45, 62
Hart-Celler Act, 17, 46
Havana, Cuba, 30
Hendricks, Glenn, 57

Henríquez, Noel, 29
Hernandez, Julio, 68
Heureaux, Ulises, 27
Hispaniola, 15, 16, 21–25, 41, 42

Immigration Act of 1924, 46
Immigration and Nationality Act of 1952, 17
Immigration and Naturalization Service (INS), 14, 18, 39, 40, 41, 44, 45, 58
Immigration Reform and Control Act, 18
Ingenio Santa Fe, 97
International Monetary Fund, 35
Inwood, New York, 62
Irish, 62, 63

Jamaicans, 62
Jews, 62
Jiminez, Miguel, 69
Johnson, Lyndon, 33

Kenya Hand Made Cigars, 65
Knapp, Captain Harry S., 28

Labor, Department of, 48
Laguna Verde, Dominican Republic, 87
Latinos, 15
Lower East Side, 64

Manhattan, 16, 62, 64
Manhattan Valley, 64
Marichal, Juan, 87–89
Martinez, Antonio, 65, 66
Matrimonio de favor, 79
Matrimonio de negocio, 80
Medicaid, 79
Merengue, 19, 63, 71, 72
Mexico, 17, 18, 23, 41
Miami, Florida, 37, 38, 61, 72, 106
Middle Ages, 21
Migration Today, 78
Mona Island, 42

Mona Passage, 38, 41–43, 45
Mulattoes, 25, 57

Nagua, Dominican Republic, 43
National Army, 29
Nevárez, Luis Rolón, 44
New Jersey, 41, 62
New York City, 15–18, 30, 38, 47, 59, 61–63, 65, 66, 69, 72, 77, 78, 79, 80, 83, 106
Nicaragua, 13
Northern Manhattan Coalition for Immigrant Rights, 63, 67
North Tarrytown, New York, 69
Nouel, Archbishop Adolfo A., 27

Panama, 37
Paraguay, 14
Paris, France, 72
Patrón, 30
Perez, Alilio, 58
Perez, Moses, 63
Personalismo, 27, 72
Peru, 23
Philip II, king of Spain, 22
Philip III, king of Spain, 23
Pico Trujillo, 13, 14, 15
Puerto Ricans, 15–18, 41, 42, 62, 64, 74, 106
Puerto Rico, 16, 30, 38, 41–45, 47, 88, 106

Queens, New York, 16, 64

Ramey Air Force Base, 45
Reformist party, 19
Regina Express, 37, 38–41
Renta, Oscar de la, 106
Reyes, Reyna, 35
Rincón, Puerto Rico, 43
Roman Catholics, 57
Roosevelt, Theodore, 27

Sabana Iglesias, 57

Saint-Domingue, 24, 25
Saint Martin, 45
San Juan, Puerto Rico, 41, 44, 61
San Pedro de Macorís, Dominican Republic, 85–87, 97–100
Santana, General Pedro, 27, 28
Santo Domingo (city), 13, 16, 22, 23, 33, 37, 61, 62, 86
Santurce, Puerto Rico, 41
Somoza, Anastasio, 14
Soto, Mario, 93–96
Spain, 22, 24, 25
Spanish, 21, 23, 25, 48
Sport, 91
Sporting News, The, 91
"Stop 15," 41
Stroessner, Alfredo, 14
Sugar, 28
Sunset Park, New York, 64

Taino Indians, 23
Tavarez, Félix, 38, 40
Tetelo Vargas Stadium, 100
Texas, 41
Tributario. See Visa broker
Trujillo, Generalissimo Rafael Leónidas (Jefe), 13, 26, 29–34, 57

United States, 14–18, 21, 27–29, 31, 33, 34, 38, 39, 41, 42, 45–48, 57, 58, 61, 66, 67, 73–80, 82, 87, 96, 101, 102, 105, 107
U.S. Marines, 28
University of Santo Domingo, 22

Valverde, Dominican Republic, 38
Visa broker, 47
Visas, 18, 46–48

Washington Heights, New York, 16, 62, 63, 68
Western Hemisphere Act, 17, 46
Wiarda, Howard J., 26
World Series, 91

PICTURE CREDITS

AP/Wide World Photos: pp. 15, 29, 32, 34, 35, 36–37, 40, 45, 49, 50, 51, 95, 97, 100; Bibliothèque Nationale, Paris: p. 25; Neal Boenzi/*New York Times*: p. 68; Carrie Boreta/*New York Times*: p. 86; Cincinnati Museum of Art: p. 22; Jim Estrin/*New York Times*: p. 107; Ethnic Folk Art Center: p. 72; Danielle Fauteux/Amstock: p. 77; Angel Franco/*New York Times*: p. 44; Rocco Galatioto: pp. 70–71; Milton Grant/United Nations: p. 12 (neg. # 155128), p. 18 (neg. # 155129), p. 59 (neg. # 140728), p. 75 (neg. # 150258); Immigration and Naturalization Service: p. 47; Library of Congress: pp. 20, 23; Keith Meyers/*New York Times*: p. 67; Hakim Mutlaq: cover, pp. 52 (top), 53, 54, 55 (top, bottom), 56, 64, 81, 82; *New York Times* Pictures: p. 60; OAS: pp. 31, 41, 42, 73, 84–85; Katrina Thomas: p. 52 (bottom); UPI/Bettmann Archive: pp. 16, 33, 89, 90, 104–5

CHRISTOPHER DWYER is a free-lance book and magazine writer and consultant. He holds a B.A. in economics from Columbia University.

DANIEL PATRICK MOYNIHAN is the senior United States senator from New York. He is also the only person in American history to serve in the cabinets or subcabinets of four successive presidents—Kennedy, Johnson, Nixon, and Ford. Formerly a professor of government at Harvard University, he has written and edited many books, including *Beyond the Melting Pot*, *Ethnicity: Theory and Experience* (both with Nathan Glazer), *Loyalties*, and *Family and Nation*.